It was him. The man who haunted her most sensual dreams...

Emma thought, staring at Burke Buchanan as he stood a few feet away. Flesh and blood. *Clay's younger brother.*

Emma's gaze connected with Burke's as she studied his face, recognizing every masculine detail. His long, fine-bladed nose flared slightly, as if he'd caught her scent. He was younger than she'd imagined he would be. But there was no denying that he was all man, with no hint of immaturity.

Suddenly, Burke reached down and picked up her suitcase. "I'll take this for you," he said as he began to walk toward the waiting car.

Emma was about to insist that she could get it herself, but she would have been talking to his broad back. Instead, she followed wordlessly, wondering just what the hell she had let herself in for....

Dear Reader,

It wouldn't be summer without romance, or June without a wedding—and Special Edition brings you both this month!

Our very romantic THAT'S MY BABY! title for June is *Happy Father's Day*, by Barbara Faith. In fact, this daddy has *six* adopted children he calls his own! Now he has to convince the woman of his dreams to become part of his family.

What would June be without blushing brides? Well, first we have book two of Christine Flynn's miniseries, THE WHITAKER BRIDES. In *The Rebel's Bride*, it's renegade Caleb Whitaker's turn to walk down the aisle. And *Waiting at the Altar* is where you'll find ever-faithful Jacob Matthews—this time, he's determined to be a groom at last in book two of Amy Frazier's series, SWEET HOPE WEDDINGS. In Gail Link's *Marriage-To-Be?* the nuptials are still in question—it's up to the bride to choose between two brothers.

Rounding out the month are two authors new to Special Edition. Janis Reams Hudson has a sexy tale in store when two sparring lovers issue the challenge, *Resist Me if You Can*. And after Lois Faye Dyer's *Lonesome Cowboy* meets his match in a spirited schoolteacher, his lonely days just might be over.

So don't miss a moment of these wonderful books. It's just the beginning of a summer filled with love and romance from Special Edition!

Sincerely,

Tara Gavin,
Senior Editor

Please address questions and book requests to:
Silhouette Reader Service
U.S.: 3010 Walden Ave., P.O. Box 1325, Buffalo, NY 14269
Canadian: P.O. Box 609, Fort Erie, Ont. L2A 5X3

GAIL LINK

MARRIAGE-TO-BE?

Published by Silhouette Books
America's Publisher of Contemporary Romance

To Keanu Reeves: a talented actor who is a joy to watch.
Thanks so much for the inspiration.

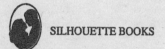 SILHOUETTE BOOKS

ISBN 0-373-24035-X

MARRIAGE-TO-BE?

Copyright © 1996 by Gail Link

GAIL LINK

A bookseller since 1977, Gail Link realized her dream of becoming a published author with the release of her first book, a historical novel, in 1989. *Marriage-To-Be?* is Gail's sixth published book and her first for Silhouette—and her first contemporary novel.

Gail is a member of the national Romance Writers of America and Novelists, Inc. She has been a featured speaker at many writers' conferences, and several publications have featured her comments on the romance genre, including *Publishers Weekly* and *Romance Writers' Report*. In 1993 Gail was nominated for the *Romantic Times* Reviewer's Choice Award for Best Sensual Historical.

In addition to being a voracious reader, Gail is also an avid musical theater and movie fan. She would love to hear from her readers, and you may write her at P.O. BOX 717, CONCORDVILLE, PA 19331.

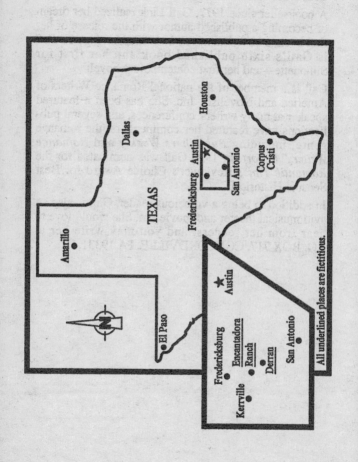

Texas map showing: Amarillo, Dallas, El Paso, Fredericksburg, Austin, Houston, San Antonio, Corpus Cristi

Inset map: El Paso, Fredericksburg, Kerville, Encantadora Ranch, Derran, Austin, San Antonio

All underlined places are fictitious.

Prologue

It was a simple scene, clean and uncluttered. Raw power radiated from both central figures. The spirit of the pair was tangible, alive and incredibly virile. Lean muscles of man and beast rippled in the molten glow of the dazzling sunset. On each was stamped the emotion of pure triumph. Neither was giving way; each retained his pride, recognizing the force, the power of the other, a mutual consent of purpose. The rider wore only tight-fitting jeans, one fist raised high in the air. The huge, brown-and-white paint horse wore only a bridle, his strong back legs supporting his flailing front hooves.

Swallowing what remained of the neat bourbon in his glass, Burke Buchanan leaned back in his comfortable leather desk chair, narrowed his dark brown eyes and stared at the large oil painting that he'd just hung in his office.

Fitted into the bottom of the dark wood frame was a brass plate engraved with the title of the painting. The name the artist had given it was honest, direct: *Untamed.*

A small smile of pleasure flitted over Burke's lips, thinning them slightly.

Damn Clay! he mused. Not only had his older brother sent him the perfect birthday gift—though it was a bit belated—he'd also sent him a puzzle.

Burke had felt an affinity with the painting as soon as it was uncrated, a private feeling of revelation that he couldn't share with anyone else. The man portrayed there bore an uncanny resemblance to himself, and yet it wasn't actually him.

He lifted himself from the seat, walking closer to the work. It was as if the artist had a pipeline to his soul and had translated that to this canvas. Internal became external. Hidden strength became visible energy. The mutual respect of man and beast became a thing of primal beauty.

Burke read the name of the artist: Emma Cantrell.

A sigh of puzzlement escaped from his lips.

A sigh of discontent escaped from her lips.

Emma paced back and forth across the bare wood floor of her studio. Sunlight filtered into the room, striking the canvas on display. She paused before it, arms akimbo, her head cocked to one side, her lips twisted in a wry grimace. Something was missing, and she couldn't figure out what.

She paid no attention to the two larger paintings that rested against the far stone wall; they were finished and ready to be added to those already shipped to the Barton Gallery in Houston, where she would be having an exhibition later in the month. Instead, Emma focused on the picture before her. It was an illustration for an upcoming book, an historical romance novel by a bestselling writer. She did all of Kate's covers, and this was to be the first hardcover, so Emma wanted it to be especially unique.

Minutes passed.

It was no use, Emma discovered. She just couldn't concentrate on the job at hand.

What was really bothering her, she decided, was something she'd done and now couldn't undo.

Selling a painting was an everyday occurrence for a successful artist like herself. It was how she earned her living.

But why that one? *Why had she sold it?*

A moment of weakness?

A moment of fear?

The question disturbed Emma. What did she have to fear from a painting? she chided herself. Not a damn thing!

Deciding that her brooding wasn't doing her any good, she removed the paint-splattered blue smock that protected her T-shirt and jean shorts and tossed it to one side, where it landed on a low wooden bench. Then she left her studio, shutting the door carefully behind her, determined to put thoughts of *that* painting out of her mind.

Easier said than done, she discovered as she entered her house. It, too, was made of stone, with high ceilings and a spectacular view of the mountains from the living-room window. Emma never tired of looking at such beauty.

She poured herself a large glass of iced tea and decided that she would read for a while. Maybe that would relax her.

She had completely forgotten about the miniature she'd hung on the wall near the fireplace. But when she plunked herself down on the comfortable sofa and curled her legs up under her, she saw it.

Ordinarily Emma used a sketchbook, creating snatches of ideas rapidly worked out in pencil for a rough draft of a painting. But this work hadn't needed any planning.

For far too many nights the image of the man and his horse had haunted her dreams, finally forcing her to exorcise their presence by putting them on canvas. After completing the small picture, she'd found that her vision couldn't be contained. She'd set the miniature aside and redone the painting on a much larger canvas.

Rising, Emma made her way to the miniature. Her hands trembled as she reached out, lifting the framed piece from the wall.

Had she really painted that expression of indomitable pride on the cowboy's face? Was it only her imagination, or did he possess a sensuality that compelled?

No, it wasn't her imagination, Emma conceded. His image did entice her. In dreams and waking, on canvas, in crowds or alone. He was *her* image; she was *his* prisoner.

And she'd built the jail with her own dreams. Like Pygmalion, she'd fallen in love with her own creation.

Selling the painting hadn't lessened her fascination with the man. If anything, he haunted her even more.

Chapter One

"So, what brings you to Houston, little brother?' Clay Buchanan asked, saving the material on his computer with a click of the mouse. Rising from his chair, he walked around the massive walnut desk to hug the other man who had just entered. "And," he continued, "how long are you planning to stay?"

Burke returned his older brother's effusive greeting, then eased his lean frame into the butter-soft leather wing chair that flanked one side of his brother's desk. His glance took in the formal English styling of the room, from the hunting prints on the walls to the furniture. It certainly was a definite contrast to his own informal office at the ranch, Burke thought. This room suited Clay's sophisticated tastes.

"I came to pick up one of Jessie's birthday presents," Burke replied. "So I'm just in town for the day."

"Too bad," Clay said, returning to his seat behind the desk, "or I could have invited you to join me tonight for dinner. There's someone special I'd like you to meet."

Burke raised one dark brown brow. "Special? As in a *woman* special?"

Clay smiled. "Right on target, Burke," he admitted.

"Who is she?"

Clay heard the skeptical note in his voice. "The woman I want to marry."

The only visible reaction from the other man was a slight flaring of the nostrils of his fine-bladed nose. "Are you sure it isn't just your hormones talking?" Burke asked in a cynical voice.

"My God, Burke," Clay admonished with a direct stare, "this isn't about sex."

"Are you telling me that you're in love with this woman?"

"I think I am."

"Think?" Burke asked in a scoffing tone. "Or is it that *she* wants you to think you are?"

Clay sighed. "Not every woman is the manipulating, scheming bitch that your wife was, Burke," he said.

"No, I don't suppose they are," Burke replied casually. "But you have to admit, when most women hear the name Buchanan, they tend to see dollar signs."

"Emma isn't like that," Clay retorted.

"How can you be certain?"

"You'd have to know her," Clay said. "She's fiercely independent, with an important career of her own. My money and position are of little consequence to her."

Burke rose from his seat and walked the few feet to the low table that held a bottle of bourbon, a bucket of ice and several glasses. He picked up the silver tongs and plopped several cubes of ice into a crystal tumbler, then poured in a generous splash of the amber liquid. He tossed back the drink with one swallow.

"How long have you been seeing her?"

Clay watched his younger brother, noting the stiff set of Burke's shoulders beneath his denim jacket. Once again Clay silently cursed the girl who'd robbed his brother of happiness and dreams all those years ago. Her false promises and declarations of love had soured his brother on romance, had crushed his trusting nature. If only Burke hadn't been so young, barely seventeen; if only he'd had a chance to experience more of life before being ripped apart emotionally by a conniving woman out for the most generous payoff she could get.

"Six months, more or less," Clay answered.

"So what's the rush?" Burke set down his glass and wandered over to the large bank of windows, staring down at the minuscule people in the street far below. So many buildings, so much confinement in this concrete cage. Burke preferred the wide-open spaces of the ranch to this urban nightmare. The city was Clay's territory, just as the Encantadora was his.

He turned and faced his brother, an ugly suspicion entering his mind. "She's not pregnant, is she?" Burke would hate to see his brother taken advantage of as he had been, especially with such an old trick.

Clay sat back down in his chair. "No," he said, shaking his head. "Emma's not pregnant. In fact," he confided, trusting his brother with the information, "I've never even slept with her."

At this comment, Burke stared in amazement. He could hardly believe what he was hearing. This, from his eldest brother—a man, Burke knew, who enjoyed the delights of female company and all the fringe benefits of such.

"Hard to believe, isn't it?" Clay responded with a smile. "But Emma's not a woman to enter into relationships lightly, I've discovered. I respect that."

Burke wondered if this Emma was playing his brother for a fool. Clay liked the company of women. Anyone familiar with Houston society knew that for a fact. Clay was a Buchanan, with a Buchanan's appetites—those same appetites that Burke had succeeded in ruthlessly pushing far into the background so that they could never be used against him again.

"Perhaps by playing hard to get she's forced you into making this decision?"

Clay's mouth thinned in annoyance. "No," he stared firmly. "That's not Emma's style at all. She's one of the most honest women I know. When you meet her you'll see for yourself."

"I told you that I can't stay for dinner," Burke repeated.

Clay shrugged his shoulders. "That doesn't matter," he said. "I've invited Emma to spend Thanksgiving at the ranch with us. It's important to me that she meet my family. I want her to feel comfortable with all aspects of the Buchanan heritage."

Burke fixed his glance on Clay. "Have you spoken to Mama about this?"

"You know Mama," Clay said. "What's one more person at the table?" He laughed. "Of course I talked to her about inviting Emma," he insisted, his face taking on a more sober mien. "She's anxious to meet her. In fact, I told Emma that Thanksgiving is a special holiday for our family, and that this year Jessie's birthday falls on that date."

Burke smiled at the thought of his daughter, who would be turning twelve in a few weeks. He loved his child with a deep and abiding wonder. She was the one miracle that had come out of his disastrous teenage marriage.

"Emma's an only child, so I warned her that the Buchanan clan can be quite something when taken all together."

"That's putting it mildly," Burke remarked. He glanced at the slim leather watchband encircling his strong wrist. "Time for me to go," he said, taking his brother's hand. "I'll look forward to meeting this woman of yours."

Clay gave a hearty laugh. "Don't let Emma hear you say that," he chided his sibling. "She's very much her own person, Burke. Just you wait and see."

Burke sped along the deserted roadway, his thoughts returning to the conversation he'd had with his brother. Who was this woman who'd managed to capture Clay's heart so quickly? A very sophisticated lady, he would guess; one who would enjoy the comforts and distinct pleasures to be found in the fast lane. She probably belonged to the right country club, worked out in the most fashionable gym, wore the best designer clothes to cover her ultraslim body. Cool, witty and elegant, with nary a hair out of place. And blond. Icily so.

Clay had said she had her own money.

Burke's wide mouth twisted in a mocking smile. Well, there was money, and then there was the Buchanan fortune. People were always eager to get a share of it, if they could. If anyone knew that for an indisputable fact, it was he. Painfully so.

Burke eased his booted foot off the gas pedal slightly when he saw the speedometer creep up over seventy. Consciously relaxing, he changed the CD, letting the sounds of a classical guitar fill the Jeep Wagoneer. He could feel the tension easing out of his body as he listened to the performer skillfully bringing forth magic from the instrument.

Clay preferred the cool rhythms of jazz. His middle brother, Drew, liked Springsteen and classic rock. What about Clay's intended? What sort of music touched her?

Or, Burke mused, maybe nothing touched her. Obviously Clay hadn't—physically, anyway. And that was a surprise.

He really hoped that his brother wasn't making a monumental mistake, one that could cost him dearly— not so much monetarily as emotionally.

"I don't know what to say," the woman answered, staring at the ring in the velvet jeweler's box. It was an engagement ring—undoubtedly—with a flawless, emerald-cut diamond set in gold.

"You could say yes," Clay prompted, refilling the fluted champagne glass. They were seated at the best table in one of Houston's finest and most elegant French restaurants, famous for its four-star cuisine.

"No, I'm sorry, but I can't," she replied. She snapped the lid shut, pushing the box back across the table.

"Why not?"

Emma responded as honestly as she could to his question. "It's not because I'm not tempted, Clay. I am. Very much so."

"But you can rise above this particular temptation, is that it?"

Emma smiled fondly at the handsome man sitting across from her. He was charming, intelligent and good company—the kind of man mothers everywhere wanted for their daughters. She did care about him, only she didn't know if she cared enough to marry him. Emma didn't want to be married just to say that she was, as if she had no other plans in her life, or for convenience's sake because someone else thought it was long past time. What she wanted was a lifetime commitment. She wanted complete trust. She wanted—what? The passion of the ages? The promise of love everlasting?

Exactly.

"You wouldn't want me to agree just to placate your ego, now would you, Clay?"

He smiled. "Well . . ."

It was Emma's turn to laugh softly. "I think I know you better than that. You want a woman with no hesitations, no reservations about the choice. I can't give you that just yet."

Clay reached out, picked up the box and put it back in the pocket of his black dinner jacket. "I'll ask again, you know."

"Please do," she responded. "I'm flattered to know that you care, Clay."

"Is there someone else?"

Emma shook her head. "No," she answered truthfully. To herself, she added, *No one to actually speak of, for how can you discuss a man who exists only in your imagination?* The dark stranger of her dreams. The haunting specter of her ideal. A man of earth and fire.

"You're the only man I've been seeing for quite a while, Clay. My social calendar," she said with a smile, "hasn't exactly been booked solid."

"More from your choice than from want of men trying, I would wager."

"How flattering."

"It's the truth." He reached across the table and took hold of Emma's hand. "Yesterday at the gallery I saw several men watching you quite closely. And why wouldn't they?'' he demanded. ''You're a beautiful woman, Emma.'' Clay observed the color that suffused her cheeks at his compliment. He lifted his hand and ran his index finger along her cheekbone. Her pale, blue-green eyes sparkled like polished aquamarines. Emma's striking eyes were set off perfectly by her hair, a rich dark auburn. ''There are quite a few men who'd like to be in my shoes right now.''

She returned the compliment. ''And quite a few women, I dare say, who'd be very happy to push me out of this chair so that they could be with you.'' Emma sipped at her champagne. ''There's no one I want to be with right now except you,'' she conceded.

''Then I'll settle for that,'' he agreed. ''At least for the present. Do you mind if I ask you a rather blunt question?'' He proceeded without waiting for her reply. ''Do you find me attractive?''

Emma laughed again, giving Clay an arch look. ''Of course I find you attractive, Clay. I'm an artist, remember? Appreciating beauty of any kind is part of who and what I am.''

''You make it sound so clinical,'' he remarked.

''That's not what I meant.'' Emma picked up her goblet and took another sip of her champagne, enjoying its crisp, dry flavor. It was an excellent vintage. Although she enjoyed it, she would have been just as content with a cold beer. A sliver of a smile broke across her lips. She could well imagine the waiter's reproof should she ask for a cold draft.

''You're a very handsome man, and you know it,'' she teased Clay. ''Weren't you recently named Texas Bachelor of the Year by *Lone Star Monthly* magazine?''

''I didn't know you paid attention to things like that.''

"Normally, I don't," she said. "But a friend of mine, Kate Reeves, mentioned that she'd read it."

"The romance novelist?"

Emma smiled. "Now I'm impressed. Quite frankly, I'm surprised you know her." She gave him a curious look. "Do you read romance novels?"

"No," he responded. "I don't have much time to read any books, let alone romance novels. My mother, however, is a big fan of Kathryn Reeves." Clay drained the rest of the champagne in his glass. "Speaking of my mother, I can't wait for her, and the rest of the family, to meet you."

"What have you said to your family about me?"

"I told Mother that I was hoping to bring you to our ranch as my prospective bride."

Emma nibbled her bottom lip. "You didn't!"

"I did," he acknowledged. "Why not? I want them to know you're a very special person in my life, Emma."

"What about the rest of your family?"

"Ah," he drawled. "That's where the fun comes in."

"I'm not sure I like the sound of that," she said, arching her brows.

"You will," he assured her. "We have a very large family, what with aunts, uncles and cousins, not to mention my own two brothers and a niece."

"Exactly how many people live on the ranch now?"

"My parents, my youngest brother, Burke, and his daughter, Jessie. My other brother, Drew, is a journalist, and he's off in England now, visiting some of our relatives there."

"What about Burke's wife?"

The muscles in Clay's face tightened visibly. "He's divorced from her."

Emma couldn't help but notice the coldness that crept into Clay's voice when he mentioned Burke's former wife. "How old is your niece?" she continued, changing the topic.

Clay's features brightened at that question. "She'll be twelve in just a few weeks. You'll adore Jessie. Everyone does."

"Especially her uncle," Emma observed.

"You bet."

"And what about your brother?"

Clay paused for a moment as the waiter arrived with their entrées. Then he answered, "Burke is Burke."

"What's that supposed to mean?"

"My brother is a complex man, Emma."

"You make it sound like a warning," she observed as she cut into the thick piece of filet mignon before her, savoring the taste of the peppercorn sauce.

Clay considered his answer for a minute. "It is, in a way."

"Why?" She lifted the glass of cabernet sauvignon that the wine steward had just poured. Emma suspected that it was another superb vintage, reserved for the restaurant's best customers.

"Burke is very protective of the family."

"You mean he's suspicious of strangers?"

"*Cautious* is more the word I'd use," he stated.

Emma shrugged her slim shoulders. "I've got no problem with that."

"Good. I want you two to get along. Burke's the one responsible for keeping the ranch running smoothly since our father retired several years ago."

"Does that meet with your approval?"

"Yes," Clay said without hesitation. "I love the place, but it's not in my blood the same way that it's in Burke's.

Drew and I used to joke between us that if Burke were ever in need of a transfusion, it would have to be Encantadora soil."

"One tough hombre, eh?"

"He's had to be."

"Why do I think there's more to that comment than meets the ear?"

"Probably because you're right," Clay admitted. "But enough of Burke." He fixed her with a direct gaze. "How long must I wait?"

"For what?"

"To ask you again to marry me," he said with a grin.

Emma couldn't help but laugh. Clay Buchanan was a very determined man. That didn't surprise her, for she knew of his reputation in the world of business. Dating him had given her a great respect for his keen mind and savvy instincts. But it wasn't the cool, corporate executive who was wooing her—it was the man. She suspected that Clay was used to a more physical relationship than what he shared with her. Kisses were a prelude, for him, to a deeper level of sharing. For her they were a pleasant exchange. So far, no man's kisses, as nice as some had been—or as good as Clay's were—had sent Emma beyond herself, beyond what she imagined a kiss could be.

"Emma?"

She shook her head. "I'm sorry, what were you saying?"

"How much more time to you think you'll need to make up your mind?" he prompted.

"Ask me again on New Year's Eve."

"That's a deal."

Later that night, as Emma sat in her comfortable hotel suite, replete from dinner, mellow from the wine and unable to sleep, she reached for her sketchbook. Flipping open the cover, she picked up a soft lead pencil and started to draw.

It came as no surprise to discover the subject of her art. It was *him*—her fantasy creation.

Emma took something that Clay had said about his brother and molded it to her purpose. She sketched the man, his back to her, looking over his domain. He stood tall and proud, with the land stretched far and wide before him. Below the outcrop of rocks, a herd of horses grazed. From his vantage point, he could hear echoes of the past, see the promise of the future.

Next to the sketch Emma scribbled notes about colors and other details she wanted to add when she put this picture on canvas.

She already had the title: *The Texan.*

She sighed, closing the sketchbook. Right now she wished she were back in her own home instead of this fancy hotel room so that she could open the doors and look out into the night, see the stars, feel the cool rush of air against her skin.

Here the windows were hermetically sealed, the rooms climate controlled. In this place there was no skylight over her bed, bringing with it a sense of wonder as she lay and watched the dawn break, or the clouds roll by, or the stars twinkle.

Emma missed her home, her things. Her pillows. Her furniture. Her books. Her tapes. In the last three weeks she'd been in New York for an opening at the DeLuca Gallery on the Upper East Side and had managed several interviews with art magazines and newspapers; then she'd flown to Seattle to arrange for a one-woman show in the New Year. After that, she'd flown back to Houston for her show here, and to see Clay.

If she married Clay, she would have to give up some part of her life for his. Exchange some segment of her world for his.

If she loved him, she could make it work.

If she loved him.

Did she?

Yes, Emma thought, she did, in a fashion.

So why the doubts?

Because she couldn't keep wondering if it was the right kind of love.

Was there a right kind of love? In today's world, was that asking too much? Emma was thirty-five years old. For a good part of those years, she'd devoted most of her time to her work, investing long hours, sacrificing a personal life. It had been her choice, and one she didn't regret. Only recently had she begun to wonder about finding someone to share her life with. She was clear about what she wanted, what she'd waited for—a love that would fill her heart the way her art filled her soul.

So far, Clay was the closest she'd come to that possibility. Yet something vital was still missing, something that made her hold back on accepting his offer.

What?

Was she being overly cautious?

Emma picked up the piece of wrapped chocolate left on her pillow. Peeling off the silver paper, she bit into the truffle, enjoying the taste of the thick creamy filling with its hint of orange. She finished the candy and got into bed, her gaze resting on the bouquet of white roses in the vase atop the desk. A fresh dozen each morning that she'd been here.

Class and style—that was Clay Buchanan.

As she closed her eyes and drifted off to sleep, Emma's mind conjured up further images of roses, except that these dreamlike blossoms were dark, a red so intense and deep they had the look and feel of velvet. Their fragrance was rich and strong, a perfume that would seduce the senses. She was surrounded by them, caught up in their beauty. A secret garden for her alone, for she possessed the only key to unlock the treasure.

Burke hung up the phone in his office with a smile on his lips. He'd called his brother half expecting to get Clay's machine, since it was almost midnight. Instead he got Clay himself.

Burke had asked the burning question—had his brother become engaged?

Clay informed him that he hadn't, that Emma wasn't ready to make her decision just yet. Since there was no other man in her life, he thought his chances of persuading her to marry him were excellent. However, she'd asked him for time, and Clay would give her that.

Time for what? Burke wondered. He leaned back in his desk chair, spinning around to stare at the painting that hung on the wall, the mellow golden light above it bathing the work in a soft glow.

He'd make it his business to find out more about this woman when she came to visit in a few weeks. If she had some grand design or scheme, he'd discover it.

If she hurt Clay, there would be hell to pay.

And the name of its avenging angel would be Burke Buchanan.

Chapter Two

"I can't wait to meet the lady that Uncle Clay is bringing home," said the young girl as she eagerly scanned the sky, searching for the private plane that would be bringing her father's brother and his girlfriend. Jessie Buchanan was excited, her brown braids flying back and forth as she twisted her head first one way, then another.

The barking of the dog beside her made the man who lounged against the hood of the Wagoneer smile. He, too, was eager to meet this woman, but for reasons different than those of his daughter. Burke Buchanan would reserve any welcome he might give until much later, after he'd had a chance to see just what she was really like, whether or not she was playing with Clay's emotions for her own gain. The rest of his family was eager to meet the woman who seemed to have brought such a change into his brother's life; they waited back at the ranch with open arms.

"Will she be beautiful, Daddy?" Jessie asked, kneeling down to wrap her arms around the big dog.

"Knowing your uncle," Burke drawled, "undoubtedly so."

"Do you think that she'll...like us?"

Burke heard the hesitant tremor in his daughter's voice. He gave her one of his rare full smiles, which transformed his darkly handsome face, giving him a more carefree air. "Darlin'," he said proudly, "how could anyone not love you?"

With that remark from her beloved father, Jessie returned his smile.

Burke was well aware that he somewhat spoiled his child, trying to make up for the fact that she didn't have a mother's presence or love in her life. He did his best to be both parents for her, never wanting Jessie to think, even for an instant, that she lacked for anything. His daughter meant the world to him.

"There it is," she cried, standing up and waving her arms in salute to the approaching plane. The dog yelped in excitement, his thick tail wagging.

"Here, Renegade." Burke called the dog to him, and the animal, hearing the command in his master's voice, trotted over to do as he was bid. "Sit," the man said, his hand ruffling the dog's silver-gray fur.

Burke watched as the plane circled the area and came back in for a landing. With the turn of the plane, his expression changed, losing the unrestricted joy, becoming cautious and reserved, harder.

What exactly were they to expect from this woman?

"Looks like Burke and Jessie have come to welcome us," Clay remarked to Emma as the corporate pilot brought the small jet in to line with the runway.

Emma marveled at the vastness of the landscape. It was rugged and unspoiled, and if there hadn't been a paved runway or a hangar sitting off in the distance, she could almost believe that at any moment a group of cowboys would come riding over the hill and the hands of time would be reversed a hundred years or more to the heyday of the Texas cattle barons and their great ranches.

Emma clung to Clay's hand as the ground got closer. She was nervous, and not just with the idea of flying in so small a plane, even one loaded with all the best equipment. It was the daunting idea of meeting Clay's family, and the importance that he placed on this trip.

She shot a quick glance at the man beside her. He smiled back, squeezing her hand.

"Don't worry," Clay admonished in a gentle tone. "They'll love you."

Emma returned his smile and looked out the window again. "My God, is that a wolf?" she asked, her eyes focused on the animal that sat beside the waiting man.

Clay chuckled softly. "Almost, but not quite," he assured her. "That's Burke's dog, Renegade. Three-quarters Alaskan malamute, one-quarter gray wolf. He's had him since he was a pup."

"Interesting," she murmured.

"Hey, not my choice," Clay admitted with a slight shrug of his wide shoulders. "But then again, I'm not Burke. Somehow, Renegade suits him."

Emma looked again at the big animal. "I'll take your word on that."

Within seconds they were on the ground and the door was opened. Clay climbed out first, helping Emma alight from the plane. She stood there and watched as a young girl, braids flying, hurled herself into Clay's waiting arms. He stood up and swung the child around, much to the little girl's delight, judging from her squeals of glee.

The barking of the dog caused Emma to turn her head, and she stared at the man standing a few feet away.

Her eyes widened; her breath caught in her chest. It was *him*. The man who'd haunted her dreams. The man who'd appeared in her recent paintings, arising, she had thought, from her own imagination. How was it possible? He was here, before her. Clay's brother. Flesh and blood; tall and lean. His long legs were clothed in tight blue jeans. Emma noticed he wore the prerequisite cowboy boots, except that his weren't for show. They had a worked-in look, as did the blue-and-cream wool jacket he wore over a faded denim shirt.

Emma's gaze connected with his. She studied his face, recognizing each detail. Lean features consisting of well-defined cheekbones, wide mouth with a full lower lip, strong squarish chin, curving brows, a longish, fine-bladed nose that flared slightly as if he'd caught her scent. He wore no hat, and Emma saw that instead of a typical modern haircut that would have brushed the collar of his shirt, his was cut short, so that it was like a sleek cap against his skull. Sunlight echoed the rich tint of sable brown.

"Emma."

She blinked and reluctantly tore her eyes away, focusing instead on the man who spoke to her.

"I want to introduce you to my favorite niece, Jessica Ann Buchanan."

"I'm your only niece, Uncle Clay," the young girl cheerfully retorted.

Clay grinned, hugging the little girl again. "That's true, Jessie girl."

Emma extended her hand to the child. "Pleased to meet you, Jessica."

"You can call me Jessie, 'cause everyone does." This was delivered with a wide smile as they shook hands. "And this is my daddy," Jessie said proudly, pointing to the man who was approaching them.

Emma swallowed, her heart beating rapidly in her chest. Clay was thirty-seven, and somehow when he'd told her that Burke was his younger brother, she'd assumed that they were closer in age. This man who now stood before her was younger than she'd imagined, though there was no denying that he was all man, with no hint of immaturity.

The two men embraced warmly, with Emma and Jessie watching.

"And this, Emma, is my baby brother, Burke," Clay teased affectionately.

"Hardly a baby, I would say," Emma countered as she held out her gloved hand.

"Burke, I'd like you to meet Emma Cantrell," Clay was saying.

At the mention of the name, Burke stiffened slightly. "Cantrell?"

His voice was smoky and deep. Emma knew Clay had a lovely speaking voice, a rich baritone. But Burke's was a shade lower, huskier and somehow just that much sexier. It was the kind of voice you wanted to hear first thing in the morning, or last thing at night.

"Yes," she responded.

Burke threw a quick glance in his brother's direction.

Clay laughed. "The same."

"What are you talking about?" Emma asked.

"My brother recently sent me a belated birthday gift, Miss Cantrell," Burke explained. "A painting that was signed 'E. Cantrell.'"

"That's me." Emma blinked, turning her attention to Clay. Only one painting had been sold recently without her knowing the name of the buyer—the one piece of artwork she'd regretted parting with. "You were the anonymous buyer for *Untamed*?"

"Yes, I was," Clay declared. "When I first saw that painting, it reminded me so much of my brother that I knew I had to have it. I didn't want a business transaction to interfere with our budding relationship, so I had the sale made through another party on the condition that my real name not be used."

So, Burke Buchanan was now the owner of *Untamed*. Emma shivered, and Clay misinterpreted the gesture.

"Hey, let's get the stuff into the car before we all freeze here," he insisted, bending down to grab his suitcase which the pilot had just unloaded, with one hand and lifting his niece into the crook of his arm with the other.

He led the way to the dark green Wagoneer as Burke and Emma both reached for her suitcase.

"I'll take that for you, Miss Cantrell," Burke said in a distinctly cool tone, picking it up and beginning to walk away.

Emma was about to insist that she could get it herself, but it would have been a waste of time, since she would have been talking to his broad back. Instead, she followed, wondering just what the hell she'd let herself in for.

* * *

Burke listened halfheartedly to the conversation in the car as he drove the few miles from the airstrip to the main house. Clay and his companion were installed in the back seat, with Jessie, in the front passenger seat, doing most of the talking. The woman was quiet, making only brief comments when called upon.

She was a complete surprise.

He'd expected a female dripping with sophistication, possessing a brittle charm, one of any number of such to be found in the circles that his brother usually frequented. Contrary to that, she appeared relaxed, with a comfortable sense of style. He'd expected a woman loaded with expensive trinkets, hiding behind a facade of designer clothes meant to impress the locals. Instead, she wore a good-quality, durable denim jacket, underneath which he glimpsed a long white shirt and dark green turtleneck. Navy leggings along with thick gray socks and lace-up boots completed the outfit.

Burke glanced swiftly into the rearview mirror. Were those wind-tossed auburn curls as soft to the touch as they looked?

What the hell was wrong with him? And where had that errant thought sprung from?

He shoved it quickly out of his mind, shifting his thoughts to something more mundane, like the road in front of him.

"Can I, Daddy?" Jessie begged sweetly.

"Can you what, darlin'?" Burke asked, knowing that he hadn't actually heard his daughter's request.

"Can I show Emma my horse?"

"That's Miss Cantrell to you, and I think that she probably has more important things to do than waste time—"

"It's Emma, and I would be happy to have a look at Jessie's horse, *Mr.* Buchanan," she interrupted quickly. "It's no bother, I can assure you. If it were, I'd let you know. Whenever Jessie wants to show it to me, I'll make the time."

"Okay, Daddy?"

"Fine," Burke agreed. He shot another glance into the rearview mirror; this time his gaze connected with that of Emma's. Clear, direct eyes of blue-green met his.

Burke broke the connection as his brother, his arm about Emma's shoulders, said, "We're here."

Emma rose from the bed where she'd been resting. Glancing at her wristwatch, she saw that it was already late afternoon. She was surprised that she'd actually fallen asleep, not realizing she was quite so tired. The hot, relaxing bath must have helped put her in a more languorous mood.

In her bare feet she padded to the oak-and-glass doors that separated the large bedroom from the en suite sitting room, and walked to the window. She parted the curtains and focused her attention instead on the room. It was lovely, decorated with a sense of welcome and ease and offering comfort with touches that appealed to her feminine nature. Two low, overstuffed chairs rested on a Chinese carpet in emerald green and rose. A secretary stood against one wall, a small fireplace opposite.

Going back into the bedroom, Emma stood and looked at the homey collage above the headboard. Mixed in among what she assumed were family photographs were assorted grapevine wreaths of different designs and shapes, mixing dried and silk flowers. Peering closer, Emma smiled at the whimsical straw hat that hung there also, decorated with twisting ivy, a bouquet of red roses and cascading green ribbons.

Her suitcase still lay open on the bare oak floor, a few items scattered within. Staring at it, and knowing she must make an effort soon to dress for the informal supper that was to take place in less than an hour, Emma found her thoughts fixed instead on the man who'd insisted upon bringing the case up to her room.

Clay's younger brother was far too disturbing. There was a slightly formal composure about him, coupled with an intensity, as if he were holding himself tightly constrained. Emma sensed some deep undercurrent waiting to boil to the surface.

She contrasted the welcome she'd received from Clay's parents, which was warm and inviting, to the rather cool, aloof one she'd gotten from Burke.

And what about her reaction to him? she wondered. What exactly had passed between them upon meeting? She'd felt the recognition, the sparks.

Or had she just imagined that there'd been something?

No. She couldn't have. It had been too acute on her part. He was so physically like her ideal, the spitting image of the hero in her paintings. Tough, self-reliant, a law unto himself, needing no one.

Burke had excused himself from the impromptu greeting in the hallway, insisting in a polite, crisp tone that it was no bother to take her luggage upstairs.

Once more their gazes had met and held momentarily.

Emma wrapped her arms about herself, wondering what exactly it was about the particular shade of brown in Burke's eyes that had held her temporarily captive.

Fathomless.

Yes, she decided, that was the word she was searching for. A woman could get lost in those fascinating eyes if she wasn't careful. They held secrets.

But what kind of secrets?

That shouldn't matter to her, Emma decided, bending down to remove a pair of flat brown shoes from her case. It was none of her business if Burke Buchanan had secrets galore. She was only here because of Clay.

She snapped the suitcase closed and stood up. That Burke resembled the man in her painting was unimportant. It was simply a fluke, an accident of circumstance. She shouldn't place any more significance on it than that.

Yet, she thought as she walked to the closet to fetch her clothes and change, Clay must have seen the resemblance immediately. He'd bought that painting especially for Burke, she was sure, because of the resemblance.

Emma shivered slightly. Burke now owned the painting. Did that mean that somehow, in some way, he owned a part of her, as well?

Burke sat in his office, ostensibly catching up on some paperwork. At least that's what he told himself. He'd been staring at the same page of figures for more than five minutes, not really concentrating. Instead, he found himself thinking of the woman his brother had brought home. The same woman who had painted the haunting picture he had come to love.

What was it about her that had this strange effect on him? Burke dismissed the unexpected allure as probably nothing significant. Just the average, normal reaction of a male to a striking female. His mother's native language had a word: *bruja*. Witch. Weaver of magic. In this instance, her weapon was an artist's brush and her imagination. Powerful tools.

Burke shoved back in his chair. Rising, he began to prowl about the room, a restlessness crawling through his skin. Suddenly, he stopped, a vivid, living canvas having leaped unbidden into his mind. He could see Clay and this woman in a passionate embrace, upstairs, in Clay's room, all defenses down, all senses alive.

Burke's hands automatically formed tight fists at his side. A burning anger coursed through his blood. A spontaneous, unfamiliar streak of white-hot jealousy rose within him.

"Burke. What's wrong?" a familiar masculine voice demanded.

He snapped his head to the side and saw his brother standing in the doorway.

"God, Burke, you look angry," Clay said, walking in and shutting the door. "What's wrong? Is there something I can help you with?"

Burke relaxed, unclenching his fingers. He took a deep, calming breath.

What the hell had happened to him?

"It's nothing," he said reassuringly.

"Well, it certainly appeared as though there was something bothering you."

"Nothing I can't handle," Burke affirmed.

"You're sure?"

"Yes," he said in a tone that conveyed he wanted the subject dropped.

Clay shot him a curious look, backing off from probing further. He knew when to push—and when to retreat. His success in the business world had taught him that. So he settled himself on the comfortable, well-worn, tan leather sofa while Burke resumed his seat behind the desk. Clay glanced at the painting that hung behind his brother and smiled proudly. "Emma's terrific, isn't she?"

"There's no denying that she's a talented artist," Burke agreed in a level voice.

"And just wait until you get to know her better," Clay said affably. "You'll see just how special she is, Burke."

"I must admit she wasn't quite what I expected," Burke said, picking up the glass of freshly brewed iced tea that sat on his desk and taking a healthy swallow.

"Boy howdy, ain't that the truth," Clay said, giving a hearty laugh. "Emma's one in a million."

"And you love her."

"Yes," Clay answered.

Burke set the glass back down, fixing his brother with a penetrating look. "But she doesn't want to marry you?"

"Emma just wants some time to be sure."

Burke leaned back in his chair. "So, how long must you wait for her to be sure?"

"Until New Year's Eve," Clay said.

"Mmm. Just a little over a month," Burke murmured.

"Precisely."

"I've never known you to fail in getting what you want, big brother," Burke commented.

"And I certainly don't intend to start now," Clay stated. "Besides," he added confidently, "I don't think that I will."

That was Clay, no doubt about it, Burke mused silently. His brother always set a course of action and followed through to its conclusion, no matter what.

"I came here now to ask you a favor," Clay said, getting Burke's attention.

"Name it."

Clay shot his younger brother an arch look. "You don't know what I want."

Burke responded, "Doesn't matter, Clay."

"Be my best man."

Burke swallowed hard. He wasn't prepared for this.

"Well?" Clay questioned. "What's your answer?"

Burke narrowed his eyes in concentration. What other rational answer could he give? "I'd be honored to stand up for you."

Clay smiled. "Thanks, little brother. That means a lot to me, just as I know it will mean a lot to Emma when she gets to know you better."

"And what about sex?"

Clay was surprised by his brother's blunt query. "What about it?"

"Are you waiting till the wedding night?"

"If that's what Emma wants, then yes, I will."

"What about what you want?"

"I'm hardly a teenager anxious for my first sexual experience, Burke," Clay said offhandedly. "I can control myself."

At that remark, Burke drew in a sharp breath.

"Oh damn, Burke, I'm sorry. That was rather tactless of me." Clay threw his brother an anxious look. "You know I wasn't referring to you and the past."

Burke shrugged his shoulders. "I know you weren't. But you can't help if that's the way it was," he said flatly, thinking back on the circumstances that had led to his own marriage. "I was young and stupid."

"No," Clay stated. "You were never stupid, Burke. Naive, maybe," he acknowledged. "What you were was carefully seduced by a clever schemer who had dollar signs in her eyes."

"We're not talking about me." Burke's hands gripped the leather arms of his chair. When he spoke, his voice was a deep, husky growl. "Do you want her?"

"Of course I do," Clay assured his brother. "How could I not want a woman like her?" He paused, his blue eyes thoughtful, a speculative look on his handsome face. "Have I thought about what it would be like to be with Emma? I've wondered more times than I care to consider. But, like I said, if I have to wait to have her in my bed, then that's the way it'll be." Clay rose. "I've got to make a few more calls before dinner." He walked to the door, saying over his shoulder, "See you in a little while."

As he made his exit, Burke barely relaxed his steely grip on the chair.

Satin. He imagined that her skin would feel like satin.

Sweet. He believed that she would taste like fresh wild honey.

Fragrant. He guessed her scent would be a blend of citrus and flowers.

Burke inhaled sharply.

This was a ridiculous waste of time, speculating on things that didn't—shouldn't—concern him. This was an aberration, one that was dangerous to pursue, even if it was only in his mind.

She was his brother's woman.

Chapter Three

Emma could barely take her eyes off Clay's younger brother. Between eating the fine meal that had been prepared for them and conversing with Clay, who sat on her right, and his father, Noah Buchanan, who sat to her left, she found her gaze often wandering to the man who sat opposite her, Burke Buchanan. Like a magnet to true north, she found it almost impossible to let a minute go by without snatching a glimpse.

Then, realizing she was being imprudent, Emma focused her attention where it belonged.

"I understand from Clay that your recent show in the Barton Gallery in Houston was quite a success."

Emma turned to the woman addressing her. Clay and Burke's mother, Santina Buchanan, was a beautiful woman in her middle fifties. With her trim shape and stylishly cut dark hair, she looked at least a decade younger.

Smiling, Emma said, "Yes, it was. You never know when you do one of these things how it will turn out, whether it will appeal to the collector." She picked up her knife and spread a dollop of butter on a thick-crusted slice of hearty rye bread. "I'm just lucky that the style of artwork that I do is appreciated by so many generous people."

"Well, if that painting in my son's office is any indication of your work, then I would say you're very talented, my dear." Noah Buchanan was a handsome man in his late fifties with a trim brown beard and a sparkle of humor in his blue eyes.

"Thank you," Emma said in response, taking a sip of her iced tea. It was the preferred drink of the Buchanans, she'd learned, no matter what the temperature outside. Having seen some of the incredible artwork their home held, she was flattered and happy that Clay's father genuinely liked her work.

'I would agree," Santina said.

Burke, Emma noted, was oddly silent. What did he really think about the painting? Had he made the connection?

From the other side of the table, Jessie asked, "Do you get paid lots of money to paint pictures?"

"Jessie Ann," Santina cautioned, "that's none of your business."

Emma almost choked on her drink. Carefully, she put the large glass down on the simple, white-linen placemat. With a grin, she chose to answer the little girl's question. "I manage to make a very comfortable living."

"What's comfortable?" Jessie demanded.

Emma laughed. "That would depend on whom you're asking, Jessie."

"I'm asking you."

"Jessie." It was Burke's turn to admonish his daughter.

Emma observed that he did it softly, in an easy tone. "It means," she explained to the young girl, "that I could buy myself the house that I've always wanted, that I can travel when and where I want to, that I can do the kind of work I want to do. It means security and being able to please myself."

Jessie cocked her head. "Just by drawing pictures?"

"It's a lot more than that, honey," Clay interjected.

"Actually," Emma stated, "it is a lot like that, Jessie. I sketch most of what I do first, sort of like..."

"A blueprint?" Burke queried, fixing Emma with his dark-eyed gaze.

She returned his look. God, why did she feel a shooting spark of electricity when Burke looked at her? Realizing she was staring again, Emma blinked. "Yes, that's right," she said. Her gaze swung from Burke to his daughter. "Would you like to see some of my drawings?"

Jessie nodded her head enthusiastically.

"Good."

"Can you make one of me?" Jessie begged sweetly.

Emma nodded in turn. "Of course I can." She smiled at the little girl, thinking how pretty the child was and how easy it would be to do a flattering portrait. Even though she'd brought along a little gift for the girl's birthday, she could work up a sketch as an added bonus in time for the celebration.

"Don't you have some homework to do?" Burke asked his daughter.

"Oh Daddy, can't that wait?"

"I don't think so, Jessie," Burke stated firmly. "Finish your dinner and then I want you to get your schoolwork done."

"But I don't have school tomorrow."

Emma watched as Burke smiled fondly at his daughter, stroking his large, slim-fingered hand across her head, brushing back a few strands of Jessie's long brown hair, which was a few shades lighter than his own. The warm smile instantly transformed his serious face, she thought. It was absolutely genuine, revealing a man capable of deep emotion and real tenderness. Those qualities were there in the intimacy of his sloe-dark eyes as he gazed at his child.

Having grown up in a single-parent household, her father having died when she was a child, Emma was touched by the scene she was witnessing. There was a genuine bond between this father and daughter—among the entire family, she'd observed in the little time that she'd been here. There was a closeness she envied. At times she'd wished that her mother had remarried and had other children, providing Emma with siblings.

"If you get it done tonight," Burke said, "then you'll have the rest of this holiday time to do what you want."

"And you can help me decorate for Thanksgiving," Santina promised.

"And for my birthday?"

Everyone at the table grinned at that remark.

"Yes, *pequeña*," Santina said with a laugh. "Haven't I promised you a very special cake for the occasion?"

"Yes."

"Then I suggest you follow your daddy's wishes and get your schoolwork completed. If you do, then you may come to San Antonio with your grandfather and me tomorrow to pick out your birthday cake. You'd like that, wouldn't you?''

"Yes," Jessie said, draining her glass of milk and scooting back her chair.

"I'll come in an hour to check on you," Burke promised as the little girl left the adults to the rest of the meal. "So no video games, okay?"

"Okay, Daddy," Jessie called as she ran off.

"Now, who's ready for dessert?" Santina asked.

Everyone at the table indicated that they were.

Since they were eating informally in the very spacious kitchen, Santina rose and began clearing away the remains of the dinner. Emma did likewise, and was surprised when the men joined in. It was a revelation to see boardroom tycoon Clay Buchanan, his rancher brother, and their father, all men of wealth and power, doing domestic chores. Within minutes the leftover food was put away and the dishes stacked in the dishwasher.

Several varieties of fresh pies were housed in the genuine pie safe that Santina opened. She brought out three and placed them on the island counter. "Who wants what?" she asked as she reeled off the list, cutting generous slices as she received their requests.

Emma served. When she set down his plate, Noah murmured a thank you, as did Clay, who couldn't resist capturing her hand in a proprietary gesture and bringing it to his lips for a kiss. "Delicious," he drawled.

Noah and Santina smiled at the flirtatious demonstration, but when Emma's gaze swiftly flew to Burke's face, she saw his wide mouth was a grim, tight line.

Hurriedly, she took her seat, a flush of heat rising in her cheeks. What was wrong with him? she wondered. Did he resent such a small display of regard between her and Clay? And why should he? Or was it that he resented her?

And then an insidious, forbidden thought brought even deeper color flooding into her cheeks. What would *his* mouth feel like on her skin? Would it be warm or cool? Soft or savage? Would it be pleasant, like Clay's? Or dangerous?

The sudden ringing of Clay's cellular phone interrupted her thoughts.

Clay answered it, immediately putting the caller on hold. "I'm sorry," he explained to the group, "but this is important. I have to take this call."

"I understand," Emma said, nodding gently as he rose and left the room.

"That's too bad," Santina said with a sigh. "I had hoped that Clay could go a day without someone needing him to handle some crisis or other."

Noah gave his wife a smile, shrugging his shoulders. "You know how much he loves his work."

"Certainly I do," Santina agreed. "But Clay needs a family of his own. Then perhaps he'll learn to take some time for himself," she added pointedly.

Noah gave a discreet cough.

Emma wondered if she were getting the official seal of approval, or if Clay's mother was just making conversation.

At his mother's remark, Burke pushed back his chair, saying tersely, "Excuse me."

Santina and Noah exchanged glances as he strode quickly from the room. His movements were sinuous, marked by a fluid easy grace, Emma noted.

The remaining adults finished dessert in silence until Clay returned. His mood was sober, and Emma knew that he didn't have good news.

"What's happened?"

He kissed her cheek and gave her shoulder a squeeze as he took his seat next to her. "I've gotta leave tomorrow morning," he announced.

"You do?" Emma ran her tongue over her upper lip. Where, exactly, did that leave her? Clay was her reason for being here.

"Do you have to go?" Santina questioned, echoing Emma's query.

"I'm afraid I do, Mother." Clay sighed. "If it wasn't an emergency, trust me, I wouldn't think of going." He poured himself another glass of iced tea from the leaded-crystal pitcher and took a healthy swallow "There's been an accident, and I have to be in San Francisco to attend a meeting that one of my people was supposed to have seen to." He addressed his father. "You remember Tom Harkins, don't you?"

"Yes, marketing vice president," Noah acknowledged.

"Well, Tom's car was involved in an accident on I-10 and he's in Houston General." At the worried looks on the faces around him, Clay hurried to reassure them. "He's okay. Only a few minor injuries. But he'll be there overnight, so that means someone's got to go in his place." He turned to Emma, taking her hand. "I'm sorry to have to run out on you just after we've gotten here, but you understand, don't you?"

"Of course I do," she insisted, covering his hand with her other one. "I'll pack my things and go with—"

"No," Clay declared. "I want you to stay here. This shouldn't interfere with our original plans. This meeting isn't going to keep me away from Thanksgiving with my family." He leaned closer to her. "Or you," he promised. "I'll fly out, do what I have to do, then come right back.'' He checked his watch. ''Tom's assistant, Linda, is faxing me his notes in a few minutes, so I'd better go and get them.''

''Why can't she handle it?'' Santina asked.

Clay turned to face his mother. ''Because Linda's new to the company, Mom. This trip with Tom was to be her first experience with one of our clients. It's too soon for her to go solo just yet. Besides,'' he added with a deep smile, ''you'd never send one of your newer assistants on an important meeting with a customer, either, would you?'' he asked, referring to Santina's highly successful interior-decorating business.

''Touché,'' his mother responded with a light laugh.

''Is she going with you?'' Emma asked.

Clay smiled indulgently as he turned back to her. ''Jealous, sweetheart?'' he teased, his large hand stroking her cheek.

Her mouth kicked up at the corners. ''I trust you implicitly.''

He kissed her mouth softly. ''Just like I trust you.''

Those words hung in Emma's memory, as if they'd been painted on the canvas of her mind. *Clay trusted her.*

But did she trust herself?

She sat alone in the den, watching the low flames in the huge stone fireplace, listening to the radio, a hits-of-the-eighties station playing softly in the background. A favorite tune of hers came on, weaving a spell over her. It was an intensely emotional song of seductive hunger and deep desire. Of passion hot and acute. Of longing so sharp it wounded the soul.

She closed her eyes, silently acknowledging that she'd never felt like that in her life. For so long she'd concentrated on her career, on her art, to the exclusion of all else. Personal relationships had taken a back seat to her creativity. She'd always depended on herself and been proud of her independence.

But now she found herself yearning for something more. It had started just over a year ago, when she'd first painted *Untamed*. Suddenly she wanted to share all that she was, all that she kept inside herself, with a man. The *right* man. A special man who would cherish the one-of-a-kind gift she'd saved for him alone. A man to strike the spark and fan the flames.

"Clay?"

Emma murmured his name, but it wasn't his face she saw in her mind's eye. The strong image that arose there was that of his younger brother, Burke.

Just conjuring up Burke's face, Emma discovered, was enough to steal her breath momentarily.

Did she dare trust this feeling, or should she discount it as a temporary aberration? Was it something that had mysteriously happened and would soon evaporate?

She couldn't deny or ignore the powerful attraction she'd instantly felt toward Burke. Without rhyme or reason it had taken hold. But had it taken root?

Emma picked up the mug of now-cooling chocolate from the low side table and took a sip.

Could she have with Clay what his parents obviously had? Even though she'd been at the ranch less than a day, Emma could tell that the affection between Noah and Santina Buchanan was genuine and deep. It was there in the little gestures, the exchanged glances, the intimate way they spoke to one another. Their love was real and lasting. Yet Emma guessed it was still very passionate.

She had to be completely sure before she could ever say yes to Clay, before she could commit herself fully to the relationship. This was too important for her not to know she was making the right decision. There could be no doubts to cloud the future. It wouldn't be fair to either of them. Hadn't that been the reason for her wanting some time to think, to evaluate their relationship?

And now the unknown factor of Burke Buchanan had been added.

Why now?

Why him?

Was it fate's idea of an ironic joke?

"I'd like you to look after Emma for me," Clay said to his brother. It wasn't a question, rather a statement of expectation.

"She's a little old to be needing a baby-sitter, don't you think?" Burke asked, a slightly mocking note in his voice.

"You know what I mean," Clay insisted with a smile, blithely ignoring his brother's sardonic tone. "I have to go on this damn trip just when I thought that I was going to get a chance to spend some time with her." He hastily repacked the suitcase he'd unpacked only hours before, adding the extra business suit he kept in his closet for just such an emergency.

"I wanted the pleasure of showing Emma the ranch," he continued with a touch of regret in his voice. "Mom and Dad will be away for most of the day with Jessie, and that means it'll be just the two of you here."

"I've got work to do."

Clay stopped what he was doing and faced Burke. "For me, Burke? Please?"

Burke took a deep breath, wishing that he had a legitimate reason to refuse his brother's request. Trouble was, he didn't. At least not one that he could tell Clay about. He wasn't about to admit that the lovely Miss Cantrell had any kind of effect on him. Such an admission wouldn't serve any useful purpose. It could only drive a wedge between him and Clay.

"Okay," he reluctantly agreed.

Clay clasped Burke on the shoulder. "I knew I could count on you."

"Just as a matter of curiosity, how old is your..." Burke paused, one dark eyebrow quirked "...girlfriend? You do know, don't you?"

Clay chuckled. "Of course I know," he said. "Emma doesn't play those ridiculous games. She's the same age as Drew, thirty-five."

Burke considered a moment before commenting. "I would have guessed she was perhaps closer to my age."

"I thought so, too, the first time I met her," Clay confided, snapping the lid on the case and placing it back on the floor. "It's that quality of innocence she has." He collected several pieces of paper from the fax machine and placed them in a leather portfolio, tossing it onto his bed. "And I don't mean just sexual innocence. No, it's something more. Maybe it has to do with her artist's imagination." He shrugged his shoulders.

He took a few steps and picked up a small wrapped box that lay on his bureau. "This is for Jessie, in case I don't get back on Thursday," he said.

"What is it?" Burke asked.

"A watch," Clay explained, handing the gift to his brother. "Something very elegant for a special occasion."

"Jessie'll love it, I'm sure."

"I hope so. Emma helped me pick it out." Clay's voice took on a more serious note. "I envy you, Burke."

Burke was surprised by his brother's words. "How so?"

"For Jessie. I want a daughter like her someday."

Burke smiled with paternalistic pride. "Yeah, she was worth every hellish moment I had to endure in my marriage with Celia."

"Hey, speaking of which," Clay interjected, "I meant to tell you, Celia divorced husband number three last week. It was in Sissy Stephen's column."

"Poor bastard," Burke remarked.

"I would imagine he was after Celia's lawyers got through with him," Clay declared.

"As long as Celia stays out of Jessie's life, I don't care what she does," Burke stated.

Clay fixed his brother with a penetrating look. "What about other kids, Burke?"

"I've got Jessie. That's enough for me."

"Suppose you marry again?"

"Look, Clay," Burke said, "I don't think that's a possibility anytime soon, so I'm not gonna worry about it."

"You never know, Burke." Clay smiled. "You could meet a woman who'll change your mind—" he snapped his fingers "—just like that. When it happens, it happens, believe me."

About an hour later, Burke, unable to sleep, decided to put the time to good use by doing some paperwork. Perhaps, he thought, he could finish what he'd started earlier and left undone. It had to be better than lying here thinking about what his brother had said.

He got out of bed and pulled on a pair of old, faded jeans and a white T-shirt, slipping his bare feet into comfortable canvas shoes.

As he made his way down the wide staircase, Burke saw a dim light below the closed pocket doors of the den. Wondering who else was awake, he went to investigate.

Sliding open the door a few inches, he peered inside. He could see that the fire was almost out. He could hear music coming from the stereo. Stepping through, he saw a figure curled up in the oversize, brown leather wing chair, a match to the one in his office.

It was Emma Cantrell, asleep.

He approached her carefully, not wanting to wake her just yet. He walked to the fireplace and banked the fire. When that was completed, he turned and moved toward the chair. Hunkering down, he stared at Emma for a few minutes, studying her features. He watched the rise and fall of her chest with each breath she took. The cream sweater she wore outlined every delightful curve. He studied the fan of her auburn lashes against the paleness of her cheeks. He observed the line of her legs, clothed in rusty brown chinos, and the patterns of the tiny roses in her socks.

Burke inhaled the scent of her perfume, the same one she'd worn earlier. It didn't take much to speculate if that fragrance would cling to a man's pillow, or to his skin, a constant reminder of the female who wore it.

Yearnings long stifled rose to the surface, making him feel edgy, restless. Like a wild mustang, he envisioned bucking off the conventions that he'd lived with for years, giving in to the demanding moment.

But that was a dangerous fantasy, one he wouldn't indulge. After his bitter experience with lust masquerading as love, he'd vowed never to go through that

again. He'd learned his lesson the hard way, through
pain and betrayal. Now he ruthlessly controlled his
emotions so that he'd never be hurt or made a fool of
again.

Empty pleasure wasn't worth the sacrifice—or the
time.

Burke wondered how far his brother's love for this
woman went. All the way to the bone and beyond?

Yet hadn't Clay recently admitted to him that he
didn't really know?

Emma moved slightly, and Burke reached out his
hand as if to caress her skin, then thought better of it. He
had to wake her up and get out of this room. It was too
intimate in here, too inviting.

And far too dangerous for his peace of mind.

He touched her shoulder gently, shaking it softly.
"Miss Cantrell."

Emma heard a deep voice summoning her from sleep.
It floated as if on the wind, wrapping around her. It was
comforting and seductive at the same time.

Yielding to the soft command, she awoke.

Emma blinked. She was in the chair, and there before
her, practically surrounding her, with one hand splayed
on the wide arm of the chair, the other resting alongside
her head on the tufted leather, was Burke Buchanan.

"I must have dozed off," she said, her voice husky
from sleep.

"It would appear so," he conceded, levering himself
up and stepping back from her.

Emma breathed a small sigh of relief. He loomed there
in the room like a dark angel, his golden skin contrast-
ing with the stark whiteness of his T-shirt. The garment
molded his long torso, revealing that although Burke was
lean, his frame was muscled. He didn't have the overly

pumped physique of the gym rat; his was that of a classic statue, smooth and sleek. She could see his hard male nipples outlined by the clinging cotton of his shirt. She almost stretched out her curious hand to feel them.

Her tongue slipped out and wet her lips as she observed the trail of a prominent vein in his upper arm, followed it to the inside of his elbow. There was strength there, evidence of the rigors of ranch work. A sculpture in marble would do justice to the play of skin over sinew. Renaissance artists would have fought over the privilege of doing such a piece.

Her eyes fell to the wide bracelet Burke wore on his left wrist, visible now that he wore a short-sleeved shirt. It was Native American design, rough-textured gold with a large, triangular lapis stone dominating the piece. She'd seen such designs before in the work of artisans like Ben Nighthorse and James Little, among others. It was bold and dynamic. Pure and strong. Assuredly masculine.

It fit him.

Emma's gaze dropped downward. The jeans he wore hugged the contours of his lean hips and long thighs like expensive gloves, outlining and defining.

She wished that she had her sketchbook.

"I'll see you tomorrow morning, Miss Cantrell."

She came out of her fog at his remark, noting the dusky shadow of beard that clung to his jaw. What would it feel like under her fingertips? Rubbing against her cheeks?

Burke was a man of textures, and as both a woman and an artist she was drawn to his masculinity. In fact, Emma honestly acknowledged, she'd never felt more female than she did admiring his maleness.

She uncurled herself from the chair and stood up, putting on her discarded shoes. She watched Burke stride to the door.

"Yes, good night," she said to his disappearing figure, tamping down the urge to run after him.

And do what? a voice asked.

Talk, she responded silently. Just talk.

Wisdom urged her to leave well enough alone. One didn't have to touch fire to know it was hot.

Burke rested his head against the wall. He'd had to get out of there before he did the unthinkable and kissed her. The urge to lay his mouth against the full softness of hers was almost overwhelming. It would have been so easy.

A low groan escaped his lips.

Paperwork forgotten, he climbed the stairs in search of a cold shower to cool his hot thoughts.

Chapter Four

Emma spread thick strawberry preserves on the slice of toast she'd removed from the silver rack, vividly recalling the scene that had taken place in her bedroom barely past first light this morning.

A knock on her door had woken her from a fitful sleep. Then a male voice had called her name.

"Emma? It's Clay. Are you awake?"

"Yeah," she responded, her voice still foggy from sleep. She scooted up against the headboard and pushed her pillows behind her, adjusting the down comforter about her waist. She licked her lips and called out, "Come in."

Clay entered, greeting her with a broad smile at the sight of her neatly tucked up on the double bed.

Emma ran one hand through the tumbled mass of curls about her head, trying to get them into some semblance of order. She'd bet that Clay was quite comfortable with ladies' bedrooms, with seeing women first thing in the morning. This was, however, a new experience for her.

She wondered what he thought of her almost-masculine attire, a loose-fitting pajama top of white cotton. It covered a pair of boxer-type bottoms, which he couldn't see. She imagined Clay was used to seeing silks and satins, expensive creations designed to stimulate and heighten a man's interest.

"God," he said, sitting down on the side of the bed, "but you're beautiful first thing in the morning."

She smiled at the compliment. "Thank you," she said, her voice husky.

"You are, you know. Honestly," he stated.

Emma could see the easy desire in Clay's eyes. It was there in the way he looked at her—as if he wanted to crawl into bed with her; as if he were waiting for an invitation.

Would Burke wait—or would he act on instinct?

Damnation! What was she doing thinking of him, especially with Clay here in her room? It was as if the specter of Clay's younger brother was here with them.

Emma frowned, realizing that Clay was talking to her and she hadn't been listening.

"So that's what kept me from joining you last night," he explained in an apologetic tone. "With so much to look over and work on, I simply forgot the time. And," he said, the expression in his eyes speaking volumes, "I didn't want to leave without saying goodbye." He moved along the edge of the bed, coming closer. "I wish I didn't have to go," he reiterated.

"I told you I'm okay with it," she assured him, reaching out her hand and taking his. It was smooth and well-kept, the hand of an executive. On one finger he wore a gold signet ring. It was solid. Tasteful. An homage to tradition. Intuitively, she knew Clay would never wear the same type of jewelry as his brother did. His tastes were more conservative, while Burke's appeared—what?—more elemental.

"I'll try and get back ASAP," he promised. "Until then, enjoy your time here at the ranch."

"I'll miss you," she said. She knew that was true; she enjoyed Clay's company. He was warm, witty, sophisticated, the kind of man she'd once thought would suit her.

"Not half as much as I'll miss you, Emma." Clay leaned over her, bracing his right arm near her hip as he brought his mouth to hers.

Emma welcomed Clay's kiss, enjoying the feel of his mouth on hers. Then, all too soon, it was gone.

"I've got to run," he said, standing up. "I'll call you later tonight." He stopped before he opened the bedroom door. "By the way, I've asked Burke to show you around some of the property today."

Emma emitted a small sigh. "I'd rather wait for you," she protested.

"Nonsense," he said with a broad smile. "Burke will do a better job than I could, anyway. Remember, this is *his* land, *his* passion, if you will...."

Emma bit into the slice of toast, her thoughts returning to the present. Small pangs of guilt racked her as she thought of how she'd made an objection, and for all the wrong reasons. Clay would think it was because she hadn't wanted to be without him instead of the real truth—that she feared being alone with Burke. Feared it because of the growing attraction she felt. This was all so new to her and she didn't know how to handle it.

Yet she couldn't broach the subject with Clay. How could she explain what she didn't fully understand herself? How could she discuss feelings that confused her?

And now Clay had made sure that she and Burke would be thrown together.

The toast began to feel dry as sawdust in her mouth, even with the generous layer of jam. Emma reached for the oversize mug of coffee and took a large swallow, wondering if there was any way she could tactfully get out of this expedition. What excuse could she use?

Nothing plausible came to mind. It appeared as though her fate was sealed.

Burke stood outside, watching Emma through the kitchen door. With the sun bright in the morning sky, its warming rays slanting through the myriad windows and skylights of the spacious room, her hair appeared touched with fire, the auburn lights glowing with a rich, inviting color.

He'd been up since dawn, early enough to see his brother, a happy smile on his face, emerge from Emma's bedroom, down the hall from his own. Clay had been so preoccupied he hadn't even noticed Burke standing in the hallway.

Had something happened between them after she'd left the den last night? Had Clay been waiting for her? Had he come to say good-night, and stayed to say good-morning?

And what if he had? Clay had every right. He wanted to marry her. Hell, they were practically engaged.

Practically, Burke thought. But not yet.

And if Clay had made love to her last night, surely he would still be there with her, sharing her bed. Nothing could have made him leave her.

Just as nothing could make Burke ignore the obligation he had to Clay to see that his girlfriend was taken care of. He'd given his word to show her around the ranch and he would keep it, no matter what the cost to him personally. He had a duty and he would carry it out. Besides, he'd spent enough time looking for an excuse to get out of it. Unfortunately, nothing was so pressing that he couldn't spare a few hours. He'd seen to it that the ranch was an efficiently run organization, and he couldn't fault it for being doubly so today.

Burke pulled open the door and walked into the room.

Emma drew a deep breath, watching Burke over the rim of her cup. In the clear light of morning, he made a powerful impression as he calmly strode into the kitchen. He said a friendly hello to Mary, the Buchanan's cook, as she handed him an oversize mug of freshly brewed coffee, then he picked up the small pitcher and poured cream into his coffee, ignoring the sugar.

Emma smiled at that. He took his morning coffee the same way she did.

"Would you like some more, Miss Cantrell?" Mary asked, holding up the pot.

"Yes, thank you," Emma replied, getting out of her chair. She could tell that the woman was about to bring it to her, and, unused to being waited on, Emma met her halfway. She put in just a splash of cream, thinking that if she stayed here longer than a few days, she'd have to buy her own supply of low-fat creamer.

There wasn't an ounce of fat visible on Burke, Emma observed, standing momentarily in place to taste her coffee. He had removed his heavy wool jacket, after pushing his well-worn suede gloves into the deep pockets, and then hung it on the back of his chair. He was dressed in a pair of faded jeans that fit him snugly, cupping his slim hips and tight rear to perfection, and a dark blue denim shirt.

Snap out of it, Emma scolded herself. It wasn't as if she'd never seen a man in jeans before. She had. Plenty. But he was different. There was no explaining why—he just was.

She joined him at the table, watching as he reached for a slice of toast. His hands were bare, his skin tanned a golden-bronze. His fingers were slim and long, with a few white marks that indicated working hands, small scars a matter of course.

"Clay asked me to show you around today," he said, pausing as he sipped his coffee. His eyes met hers over the rim. "So whenever you're ready, Miss Cantrell."

"You don't have to if you'd rather not," she insisted, stung that he continued to address her so formally. "And if I may remind you, my name is Emma."

She thought she saw a glimmer of humor light those dark eyes as he shrugged his broad shoulders. "It would be my pleasure to show you the Encantadora, Emma."

Her name on his lips sent a thrill snaking along her skin, as if he'd physically touched her with one of those long, sure fingers. She ought to come up with an excuse, any excuse, not to go.

Again, there wasn't any she could think of to do the trick, so she acquiesced gracefully. "Then I accept your kind offer...Burke."

"Mary, would you make up some sandwiches for us? Miss Cantrell and I are going for a ride, and we won't be back for lunch. Also, how about two large thermoses of your great coffee?"

"Sure thing, Mr. Burke," the cook replied, already carrying out his wishes as she delved into the capacious refrigerator and began pulling out an assortment of items. "Everything'll be ready in a few minutes."

"Thanks," he said to her. "Now," he continued, addressing Emma as he rose and drew on his jacket, "how long will it take you to get ready?"

"Ten minutes," she replied, enjoying the fluid movements he made as he slipped his hands into the gloves.

"Good," he said. "Meet me at the stables." He turned to go, then as an afterthought swiveled his head to the side and added in that deep, resonant voice, "Dress warmly. There's a real chill in the air."

"I'm hardly a hothouse plant used to having the heater cranked up all the time."

He raised a brow in skepticism. "Oh, really?"

Emma recognized the slight mocking tone in his voice, and she could see that it was mirrored in his eyes. "Yes, really," she said. "For your information, I live in New Mexico, outside of Taos, in the Sangre de Cristo Mountains. I'm quite used to cooler weather."

He was silent for a moment.

She smiled at his surprise. Served him right, she thought. How dare he assume anything about her?

A faint smile crossed his mouth.

"And I'm familiar with a horse, too," she added, rising to her full height of five feet four inches. "I even know which side to get on."

"Then we're set," he announced. "See you in ten."

Burke put the food for the excursion into his saddlebags. He waited at the entrance of the stables, a large brick-and-stone structure with a quantity of well-kept paddocks. He'd carefully chosen a mount for Emma, a pretty Appaloosa mare known for her surefootedness and even temper.

His own mount, Compañero, a four-year-old geld-ing, was a big, reddish-brown-and-white pinto. In fact, that was another thing about the painting that he found strange—the horse, except for a subtle difference in the markings, was almost a copy of his. How could she have known? He wanted to gauge her reaction when she saw it, so he deliberately brought the mare out first, his own horse remaining just inside the door to the stables.

Burke didn't have long to wait. Checking his wrist-watch, he saw that she was a minute early. He watched as she strode toward the structure. She wore jeans that hugged her feminine curves, emphasizing her small waist. A hunter green turtleneck sweater showed off her auburn hair and creamy skin to perfection. Over it she had on her jean jacket, and she wore a pair of dark green, suede gloves.

"Oh," she exclaimed as she came closer to the mare, "what a lovely creature." Emma stripped off her glove so that she could run her hand over the animal's muz-zle. The mare responded to her attentions by blowing on her fingers. Smiling, Emma reached into her pocket and produced a carrot, thrilled when the animal took the food. She stroked the mare's neck and well-groomed mane. "What's her name?" she asked Burke.

"Fancy," he responded.

"Oh yes, it fits her," Emma murmured, her blue-green eyes sparkling with excitement. "Is she for me?"

Burke nodded his head.

"Where's yours?"

Burke turned and went back inside. Seconds later, he led out the gelding and heard Emma's soft gasp. "Un-canny, isn't it?" he asked.

She stared at the animal, recognizing it instantly. "I had no idea you had a horse that looked like the one in the painting."

He could see in her eyes that she was telling the truth. There'd been no prior knowledge on her part, no grand scheme to purposefully get his brother's attention. It was all simple coincidence. If anything about this situation could be deemed simple.

"Let's get going," he said. "Do you need any help in mounting?"

Emma could feel the color rising in her cheeks, for no other reason than the manner in which he spoke. With his deep and seductive voice, he conjured up another scenario, this one fraught with sensual possibilities.

"No, I think I'll be okay," she said hastily, slipping her foot into the stirrup and throwing the other over the mare's back.

While Emma adjusted herself in the saddle, Burke checked the stirrups, making sure she had a comfortable fit. When his hand touched her jean-clad calf, he could feel the slight skittish movement she made.

Obviously, he made her nervous. Why? he wondered. She certainly appeared comfortable with Clay.

Burke's dog made his presence known then, barking excitedly.

"You don't mind if Renegade comes with us?" Burke bent and allowed the dog to greet him with a wet lick as he ruffled the dog's thick coat.

"Of course not," Emma assured him. "I like dogs."

"Then what are we waiting for?" he asked, mounting his horse and setting off.

Emma followed his lead, the animal under her eager for a gallop.

* * *

It was more than two hours later, walking their mounts so the animals could take it easy after the long, hard ride they'd put them through, that Emma finally made a comment. "Why aren't you wearing a hat?"

"What?" Burke was surprised by her question, giving her a puzzled glance.

"A hat," she repeated. "You know—" she grinned "—a real cowboy hat. A Stetson, at least."

The perplexed look on his face faded. "I'm not much for hats, cowboy or otherwise," he admitted. "Never have been." Burke reined in the paint. "I only wear them if the weather's bad, when I have to." He fixed her with his dark gaze, curiosity getting the better of him. "Why'd you ask?"

"Because every cowboy I've seen today has had on a typical hat." She waved her hand. "It's expected, you know, especially when you work on a ranch. Sort of a given, if you will."

"Maybe," he said, giving her another one of his faint smiles, more a quirk of his lips. "I don't like being typical."

Emma considered this. No, there was nothing typical about this man. He was unique. A throwback to another era in some ways, and yet a man of his time in others.

"Over there," he said, pointing to a hill in the distance, "is the border of my cousin's property. Rayburne land."

"I thought Clay told me that your mother was a Montenegro."

"She is," he confirmed. "Their land is southwest of us. Her daddy married Alicia Rayburne. Our family is pretty big, what with various branches, so we've got lots of aunts, uncles, cousins and what-have-yous, not only here in Texas, but in California, the Pacific Northwest and even overseas—in England mostly, and a few distant relations in Ireland and Wales. You'll meet several of our relatives tomorrow when they join us for Thanksgiving dinner.''

Emma mused on what it would be like to be a part of such a huge family, a family with history and roots, with traditions and memories all its own.

"Your family's been here for a long time, hasn't it?''

Burke nodded. Pride filled his voice when he spoke. "Yes. The Montenegros were a Spanish land-grant family in Texas back when Mexico still owned it. The original owner of the Encantadora was a German, Samuel Reitenauer, whose daughter married an Englishman, Rhys Buchanan. Rafe Rayburne, Texas born and bred, married Rhys's younger sister, Gillie.''

"It must be such a good feeling to know that you have a tremendous history to pass along to your daughter.'' Emma could see by the look in Burke's brown eyes that Clay had been right about his brother. Burke loved the land, all of it. The feeling was there in his voice, in his eyes, in his soul. He'd never be a man for the city, or a desk in a high-rise office complex, making the daily commute. This was where Burke belonged, just as Clay was where he belonged.

Her question to herself was where did she belong?

"You hungry?''

Burke's softly spoken query forced her attention back to the moment. Emma realized that she was indeed hungry, almost ravenous, in fact. The ride had given her a very healthy appetite. "Yes," she replied.

"Then follow me. I know a great spot where we can eat.''

Emma soon discovered that Burke wasn't exaggerating. He brought her to a lovely clearing nestled among several varieties of trees: oak, cypress and cedar, all surrounding a rushing, rocky stream. This place, she guessed, would be a riot of color in the spring and summer, alive with the vibrant hues of bluebonnets and Indian paintbrush. The green of leaves, blended with the green of grass and scrub would overwhelm them, transforming this into a spectacular oasis. In autumn it would be tinged with nature's banquet of colors, a riot of hues.

Now, however, it was touched by winter's fingers, even if the season hadn't officially started. The sun had disappeared behind several thick gray clouds. Burke's dog went scampering into the underbrush across the stream, happily chasing a fleet-footed rabbit.

Emma and Burke dismounted, and he watered the horses, then left them to graze. He handed her a thermos of coffee. "This should warm you up."

Emma unscrewed the cap, pouring the steaming liquid into the cup. It tasted divine and was just what she needed. But as for being warmed up, Emma felt that whenever Burke looked at her. A deep, sensual warmth flooded her body, tingling her toes, breasts and belly with its heat. And if it were possible, it was growing stronger with each passing moment in his company.

While she drank, Burke removed two brown paper bags and offered her one. He sat down on a large, flat-topped rock, while Emma did the same, albeit gingerly. It had been months since she'd been riding and her body was adjusting to the exercise.

She opened the bag, removing the contents, two foil-wrapped packages. She opened the largest first, finding a hearty meal of thickly sliced ham and cheese on freshly baked wheat bread. When she opened the other, she discovered it contained a wedge of pie. A linen napkin was also included.

Emma found it refreshing to be sharing a meal in such rugged surroundings, as if she and Burke were in their own private world. She silently acknowledged how risky the thought was, but it was one she couldn't help dwelling on.

"So what made you choose art as a career?"

Emma finished chewing her bite of sandwich and took a drink from her cup before she answered him. "I didn't choose art so much as it chose me," she said. "I started to draw when I was a child, doodling, sketching. One of my high-school teachers encouraged me to enter a local art contest, and I won." She smiled with pleasure, remembering her efforts. "Not first prize," she admitted ruefully, "but a solid, respectable second. Well, that work sold the day after the contest officially closed. That's when I knew that this was it for me." She took another sip of her coffee. "Before it was sort of a hobby, something I did for myself. That sale convinced me to follow my heart, and I've never regretted it."

"Were you successful right away?" he asked, his curiosity about her overcoming his determination to remain aloof.

Emma laughed softly. "Not hardly. I did some commercial art at the beginning." At his inquisitive look, she explained further. "Illustrations for paperback novels. That's how I met one of my good friends, romance writer Kate Reeves. She'd seen my work on someone else's book and asked her editor if she could have me do her next cover. Needless to say, I was flattered when the art director of her publishing house called and asked me to do it. Since then, I've done every one of Kate's covers.''

"Still?"

"Still," Emma said proudly. "I love Kate's stuff, and working with her to get the best look possible is fun. She always has great ideas that spur me on. Besides, I get to be one of the first people to read each new book. That's a real treat.''

Burke, tucking into his sandwich, didn't know what to make of Emma. She seemed sincere, a truly honest woman, one who had no hidden agendas or plans. One who appeared, at least on the surface, to have it all.

But what of love? He'd seen no hard evidence of a burning passion between her and his brother. Clay wanted her, that was for sure. But what did she want?

A rich husband so besotted with her that he offered her half his kingdom? Did she place a monetary premium on her yet-to-be-proven innocence? Was she capable of the same cruelty as Celia? The same duplicity? Lies, he knew, weren't always written on the face. Sometimes they lay hidden, festering inside until they spread their poison.

And if she was even remotely like Celia, why did he want her more with each passing minute?

"I think we'd better be getting back," he said abruptly, rising and cleaning up the remains of his lunch.

Emma heard the cool tone that had crept back into his voice. What had happened? One minute they were talking, actually having a conversation; the next, he was a hard-edged stranger once again. She could see it in the stiff set of his shoulders beneath that wool jacket.

Burke went to call his dog, then hesitated. He spied something standing a few feet away from them across the stream on an outcrop of rocks. "Look there," he whispered to Emma. With one hand, he pointed to the spot.

Emma gazed in the direction he'd indicated. An eight-point white-tailed buck stood there, watching them.

"He's magnificent," she said in a low voice, admiring the animal. Like Burke, the solitary buck belonged to the land, king of all he surveyed.

They rode back to the ranch in silence, the only noise that of Renegade's excited barking, of a flock of birds overhead. The sky was turning a darker shade of gray; the temperature had dropped fifteen degrees.

Burke knew a storm was coming.

Maybe not tonight, but soon.

A storm on all fronts.

Chapter Five

Emma walked into the house, memories of the afternoon spent in Burke's company swirling delightfully about in her brain. She had enjoyed the ride and, more importantly, the time with him. More than she should have, she admitted.

She stood with one foot resting on the bottom step of the wide stairs leading to the second floor. What was it about Burke Buchanan that drew her, that fascinated her in spite of herself? Was it that sense of self-assurance that he shared with, it seemed, all the Buchanans she'd met? Was it the easy way he spoke about his heritage, the deep affection for both his family and the land that were vital elements of his character? Or was it the gentleness that he showed toward his daughter, who obviously meant the world to him? Emma believed that Burke couldn't have been more than a boy himself when his daughter was conceived. So young for such a life-altering responsibility, a responsibility he cherished.

Or was it simply that rare smile of his that caught her unaware, a smile that muted his oftentimes somber face? A smile made all the more valuable because it was uncommon?

Whatever it was that drew her to him so inexorably, Emma realized she had to come to terms with it—and soon, before Clay returned.

"Hi. You must be Emma," said a friendly female voice from behind her.

Emma turned and came face-to-face with a woman of above-average height—made even taller by the three inch heels she was wearing. She was dressed in an elegant suit of charcoal gray wool, with a tailored, white silk blouse beneath.

"Yes, I am," Emma replied, wondering who she was.

The other woman walked closer and extended her well-manicured hand. "I'm Vicky."

At the blank look on Emma's face, the woman explained with a smile, "Vicky Montenegro, Clay's cousin."

"Hello," Emma responded, shaking the woman's hand. She could have been mistaken for Burke's twin, so alike were they in coloring.

"I stopped by to invite you and Clay to join me and my boyfriend tonight for dinner. Nothing fancy, just some regular down-home stuff at one of the local places." Vicky gave a quick look around the empty hallway. "So where's Clay?"

"He was called away on business."

"No way!" Vicky exclaimed with an exasperated sigh.

Emma gave a soft laugh. "I'm afraid so. Something came up and he had to go."

Vicky shrugged her slim shoulders. "So you're free then?"

"Well . . ." Emma hesitated, not wanting to make any arrangements just yet. "I don't know—"

"Nonsense," Vicky interposed. "It'll give us a chance to get to know one another."

"I think I should see what Mr. and Mrs. Buchanan have in mind first."

Vicky shrugged again, her straight, shoulder-length dark hair swirled about her neck. "Okay. If not dinner, then perhaps you can join us for a late drink."

"Vicky. What are you up to?"

At the sound of that deep, masculine voice, both women turned to the speaker, who stood in the hallway.

Emma guessed that Burke must have entered the house from the kitchen. She watched as the young woman greeted him warmly, giving him a hug and a kiss on his cheek. Faint traces of Vicky's deep red lipstick lingered on Burke's sun-warmed skin.

A flash of something jabbed at Emma's stomach. She recognized it as envy that the other woman could just reach out and touch Burke with ease. Envy that she could casually mark him with her mouth.

Envy turned quickly to guilt at the wayward nature of her thoughts. Mentally, she rebuked herself. *Stand back. Get control.*

"I stopped by to see if Clay and Emma would like to have dinner tonight, and find that he's away. How like Clay," Vicky added in a good-natured tone. "I just get back from a business trip and Clay's off on one. I swear, he and I hardly see each other anymore. If it wasn't for Tia Santina I wouldn't have known about Clay's homecoming until dinner tomorrow." She grinned. "And I certainly wouldn't have known about his girlfriend,'' she said, giving Emma a careful look.

''You always were a nosy little girl,'' Burke teased.

With that remark, Emma discovered yet another facet to this complex man. Standing there, she witnessed firsthand his relaxed, natural affection for his cousin. She found it spontaneous and sweetly touching, further proof that he did let some people close; that he wasn't quite as impervious to human contact as their first meeting would have indicated.

''Clay will be back for Thanksgiving, won't he?'' Vicky asked.

''He plans on it,'' Burke answered.

''Say,'' Vicky inquired, a gleam in her pansylike brown eyes, ''what are you doing tonight, Burke?''

''Why?'' His reply was made with a raised brow.

''Why don't you join us? You and Emma, that is?'' Vicky threw a glance in Emma's direction after she put the question to Burke.

Emma reacted with a start, her eyes widening. She and Burke together? With another couple? Like a date?

It was ludicrous. Impossible.

''Think about it,'' Vicky said before either Burke or Emma could respond. Lifting her arm, she checked the slim band of gold on her wrist. ''Damn,'' she said softly, ''it's later than I thought.'' She leaned over and quickly pecked Burke's cheek again. ''I've got to get a move on. Tell Santina that I'll get in touch with her later about the samples of fabrics I left for her in the den.''

Vicky extended her hand once more to Emma. ''It was great meeting you, if only for a few minutes,'' she said sincerely. ''Give me a call if you want to get together tonight. Burke has my number. It'll be fun, I promise.''

Vicky faced her cousin with a look of mock severity on her face. "And when's the last time that *you* had any fun, Burke? No, don't answer that now because it'll take too long for you to remember," she finished with a throaty laugh. "And I don't have the time to listen right now."

With that sally, she departed.

Emma watched Burke walk his cousin to the door and then outside. Anxious to put some distance between herself and the man who continued to disturb her, she mounted the stairs, mulling over Vicky's request.

A night out with Burke. An opportunity to spend even more time with him.

Was that wise, considering?

She entered her bedroom. Closing the door behind her, she leaned back against the solid wood, her hands flat against it. Drawing a deep breath, she forced herself to relax.

She couldn't.

She wouldn't.

She shouldn't.

But if he asked her? What then?

Emma edged away from the door, removing her jacket and tossing it onto the bed. She continued walking until she entered the bathroom. Getting a glass of cold water from the tap, she caught sight of herself in the mirror over the sink. Her cheeks were flushed a becoming pink, her hair was casually tossed by the wind from her ride and her eyes sparkled. She looked alive and vibrant, ready and willing to grasp at life's delights with both hands.

She took a swallow and heard a sharp knock on her door.

"Be right there," she called out, picking up a tortoiseshell comb and giving her curls a swipe. That done, she finished the water and went to answer the door.

When she opened it, Burke stood on the other side, one hand resting on the jamb. He looked down at her. "May I come in?" he asked politely.

Emma considered her limited options. What could she do—slam the door in his face? Or let him enter.

Cautiously, she stepped aside. "Sure," she responded.

He strode past her, through her bedroom, all the way into the sitting room, where he stood, waiting for her to join him.

"What do you want to do about Vicky's invitation?" He was blunt and right to the point.

Emma wanted to answer him truthfully, yet to do that she would have to reveal the dilemma she faced. One part of her wanted to say no way, that she was only asking for trouble by going with him. The other part wanted to shout yes, let's do it, and damn the consequences.

"I suppose," she began, "that we should see if your parents have any plans? I wouldn't want to upset—"

"That's not what I asked you," Burke stated, interrupting her. "If Clay were here, would you go?"

"I suppose so," she admitted, walking toward the window, her back to him for a few seconds before she turned and faced him. "It would be nice to get to know some more of your... of Clay's family."

If Burke noticed her slip of the tongue, he gave no indication. "Well, I promised Clay that I'd see to you while he was away, so in his place, I suggest that we do it."

"You don't have to if you don't want to," she stressed, believing that somehow she was forcing Burke into a situation he didn't want, a situation he wouldn't feel comfortable with. "I'm not a child who needs looking after, you know."

"No," Burke said, his dark eyes slowly dropping the length of her body and back up again, "you're certainly not a child."

A flame of heat curled in Emma's belly in reaction to his look. Suddenly, the room was too cramped, too confining. She wanted to throw open the window and let in the outside air to cool things off.

"I'll call Vicky and tell her that we've decided to join her tonight," Burke announced.

"Fine," Emma said, acquiescing.

Within seconds, she was alone, facing the consequences of her decision, along with the hotly imagined fantasies that had sprung to mind while Burke was in the room. When his gaze had skimmed her frame, she had wondered what his hands would feel like doing the same—slowly; surely, competently. What about his mouth? His tongue?

And what about him? What would his skin feel like to the touch? She wanted to chart the course of his body with her own fingers, starting from the wide forehead to the curved brows, from that strong nose to the sculpted lips, from the breadth of his shoulders down the length of his long torso and beyond.

But that's all that it was. A forbidden fantasy. A wishful daydream that hadn't a thing to do with her real life. Her own private chimera.

That's all it could be. Ever.

What had he done?

Burke asked himself that question as he stood beneath the spray of cool water in his shower, rinsing off the soapy lather from his fevered skin.

Only minutes after entering the glass-enclosed stall the wild, erotic fantasy had sprung full-blown into his brain. He'd stood beneath the water, closed his eyes and let it happen. It had been so easy to imagine other hands than his own applying the slick bar of soap to his skin. Soft, capable, feminine hands, sliding the cake of oatmeal soap up and down, around and over, back and forth. His flesh had instantly responded, becoming harder, thicker, tighter, desperately aching, craving release.

Burke turned off the water and stepped out of the shower. Grabbing a thick burgundy towel from the rack, he dried himself briskly, tossing it to the floor when he was finished. He pulled a smaller towel from the rack and used it to quickly dry his short hair.

Striding into the bedroom, he removed a pair of white cotton briefs from his dresser. As the material slid up his thighs and over his buttocks, he felt its caress like soft fingertips.

Her fingertips.

Once again, his body instantly reacted to his thoughts.

Damn! No woman had ever had this power to affect him as she did. Why, after all these years of self-imposed celibacy, did it have to be her?

And why, given that, had he agreed to go out tonight and spend even more time with her?

Burke wondered about it as he pulled on clean blue jeans and went back to the bathroom to shave.

It was all so crazy.

He realized that he couldn't pass up the chance to be with her, even if it meant sharing her with his cousin and her boyfriend. He could tell himself that he was just helping Clay, keeping his word to his brother, but Burke couldn't lie to himself as he looked into the mirror and smoothed the shaving cream across his jaw. He looked into his own eyes reflected there and admitted the truth. He *wanted* to be with her.

He stroked the razor over his neck, planning how he would act. A facade of cool indifference would be best. Polite, as the situation warranted; he had to be that. She was, for all intents and purposes, Clay's intended. A woman who might soon be as good as a sister to him. He had to keep telling himself that, over and over.

Somehow, Burke doubted he could ever perceive Emma Cantrell as a sister.

So who was she? What was she really like? Had today's outing revealed a hint of the real woman, or had it all been a clever ploy to win his favor?

And could he take her at face value? Could Clay?

"Daddy? Can I come in?"

"I'm in the bathroom," he called out in response.

He washed the traces of foam from his face as Jessie walked to the doorway of the bathroom, Renegade trailing alongside.

"Are you going somewhere?" she asked, her head cocked to one side as she watched Burke apply an expensive brand of after-shave to his face.

"You got that right, honey," he replied, holding out his arms for her as he crossed the few feet that separated them. Jessie responded instantly, hugging him close. "Vicky has asked me and Miss Cantrell to join her and Joe tonight for dinner."

She looked up, tilting her head back to see his face. "Are you taking Uncle Clay's place?"

Burke nodded, aware of the irony in his daughter's question. "In a manner of speaking."

Jessie dropped her arms and stepped away, choosing to pounce on the wide expanse of her father's bed, where she lay facing him, her chin resting on the palms of her hands. "Do you think that you'll get married again one day, Daddy?"

"Where's that coming from?" Burke asked as he finished dressing.

"Well," she explained, "my best friend in school's daddy is getting remarried and Belinda doesn't like the woman who's gonna be her new step-mom."

"You don't have anything to worry about, honey," Burke assured her.

"But what if you meet someone like Uncle Clay did? Or like Belinda's dad?" she asked with a slight frown on her face. "And what if she didn't like me?"

Burke hunkered down by the side of the bed. "I wouldn't think about marrying anyone without asking you first, Jessie."

Jessie was happily surprised with his response. She raised up and sat cross-legged on the bed. "Is that for real, Daddy? You wouldn't get married without talking to me?"

"Of course it's for real, sweetheart." Burke gave a gentle tug on one of her long braids. "Any woman I'd want to marry would have to meet with your approval before I'd consider asking her to be my wife." He leaned over and kissed the top of her head. "After all, you're my best girl, aren't you? I couldn't make a decision like that without consulting you, sweetheart."

Jessie smiled importantly, pleased with her father's answer. "Do you like Emma, Daddy?"

Like her? Burke speculated. That word was far too docile for his reaction to Emma Cantrell.

He stood and took out a pair of boots from his closet, easing his feet into them. "I think so," he replied in a noncommittal tone, placing his wallet into his back pocket. "What about you?"

"Yeah. She seems kinda neat, being an artist and all," Jessie said with enthusiasm. "And it's fun having somebody famous here, sort of almost a relative." She scrambled off the bed, leaning down to pet the big dog resting on the bare wood floor. "Can I have pizza for dinner tonight if you're going out?"

Burke gave his child a direct look. "Did you eat a good lunch?"

"Yes," she admitted.

"You're certain?" He raised a dark brow. "No extra junk?"

"Grandpa and Grandma made sure that I did," she grumbled good-naturedly, an endearing smile on her face. "Honestly, Daddy." She rolled her eyes in mock horror.

"Okay," Burke conceded with a smile. "Enjoy your pizza."

"Thanks, Daddy. I hope you and Emma have a really good time."

A good time.

What an interesting expression for his daughter to have used.

Burke wasn't sure if that were at all possible. Not while uncommon feelings of guilt rose to the surface whenever he contemplated spending time with Emma.

Emma walked into the den, deciding to wait there for Burke. She saw Santina curled up on the couch, a portfolio in her hands. "Am I interrupting?" she asked.

Santina raised her head from the page she was studying, glasses perched on her nose. "Not at all," she said, beckoning the younger woman closer. "Come on in."

"What are you looking at?"

"Fabric, paint and wallpaper samples. Have a look." She passed her the thick leather-bound scrapbook. "Tell me which one you like best."

Emma sat down next to her, glancing at the many pages filled with swatches of color and materials. "What's this for?"

"An office."

"Male or female?" Emma asked.

"Female. A doctor's office in Dallas, an OB-GYN, in fact. She and her partner want someplace that women can feel comfortable, without feeling intimidated by the typical doctor's-office decor."

Emma studied the samples closely before making her choice. They were obviously going for a warm, traditional look. She handed the book back to Santina, open to her selection.

"Interesting," the older woman said. "With your artist's eye, I was curious to see what you'd pick."

Emma's full lips curved into a smile. "So how'd I do?"

"Just fine." Santina returned the smile. "It's my choice also."

"By any chance," Emma asked, "did you do Clay's office and apartment?"

Proudly, Santina responded, "Yes, I did." She gave Emma a direct glance. "Did you like them?"

"Yes. They're both very much Clay. Reserved, yet with a good deal of charm and class." Santina had captured Clay's slightly more formal taste, somehow reflecting his impeccable manners, his inherent good breeding and underneath it all, his drive. Now Burke, Emma suspected, would be more informal, more down to earth. The colors and design he'd choose would be strong and solid, much like he was. And they would be his own.

"I've always felt," Emma said, "that good interior designers were artists who let their rooms be the living canvas of their art. Blending the client's personality into a cohesive vision of color and style."

"I'm flattered you feel that way," Santina acknowledged. "It'll be nice having another woman—another *artist,* if you will—in this family. Being the only female in the Buchanan clan, aside from my granddaughter and niece, has been trying at times." Santina placed the portfolio on the low coffee table, then removed her glasses and placed them atop it. She took one of Emma's hands, confiding, "I've always wanted to have a daughter, or even two. Maybe that's why I'm so fond of my niece, Vicky, who's been like a daughter to me. When my boys were growing up, I knew I'd have to wait until they found the women best suited to them. Then I'd have the daughters I've longed for, and they would be extra special to me because we'd have a shared love in common, that of each of my sons.

"I love my boys, Emma, and like any mother, I want them to be happy, to be loved beyond a doubt. Marriage is an important step. It can be difficult and demanding in the best of circumstances. So, please, my dear, take your time and make the right decision for both of you."

Emma wondered if Santina Buchanan could read her mind, if she could see the questions that rose to plague her. Questions that had escalated in the two days she'd been here at the ranch, questions that had intensified since she'd met Clay's younger brother.

No, of course she couldn't, Emma decided. Santina was just being a caring, concerned mother who wanted what was best for her children, even if they weren't children any longer.

Besides, it was good advice. After all, Emma had waited this long to consider marriage and a family. She had to be sure, with no shadows clouding her judgment.

"I hope you didn't mind about dinner tonight," Emma said.

"Not in the least," Santina assured her. "Vicky had already mentioned it to me when I told her a couple of weeks ago that Clay was bringing you to the ranch for Thanksgiving. She thought it would be fun to show you some of the local color. What surprises me is that she got Burke to agree to go along as well."

"I take it Burke's not quite the party animal?" Emma asked in a lighthearted tone, trying hard to keep a proper perspective on the evening.

Santina chuckled. "No," she drawled, "Burke, isn't a 'party on' kind of man. He never has been. Now my middle son, Drew, likes excitement and challenges. He's always been ready for a good party."

"He's a journalist, isn't he?"

Santina nodded her head. "Our own rolling stone."

"Your sons are all so different," Emma observed.

"Which has been an almighty blessing," said a deep, masculine voice. "It kept our house from being boring." Noah Buchanan came into the den carrying a large box. "Where would you like these, my dear?"

Santina pointed to the coffee table. "Set them down here for a minute."

Noah did as he was asked, and Emma marveled at the decorated grapevine and evergreen wreaths that lay inside the box.

"Go on, take them out if you'd like," Santina insisted. "I just bought them today in San Antonio. Aren't they lovely?"

Emma pulled out a large wreath that combined evergreen, chilies and pinecones; another was decorated with Indian corn, chilies and a combination of dried bluebonnets along with Indian paintbrush.

"Jessie picked that out for her father's office. What do you think?"

Emma held the wreath in her hands, visualizing this piece in a totally masculine room, adding just the right seasonal touch. "Perfect," she said in a soft, hushed tone, imagining what Burke's office looked like. She knew that's where her painting hung, because Clay had told her. It was then that she realized she wanted, with an almost desperate intensity, to see the picture, to see just where Burke had placed it in the confines of the room, to see where he spent so much of his time. Maybe she could even sketch him there. Capture some little piece of him grounded in his own reality as opposed to her imagination.

As if he'd stepped fresh from her mind, Burke was there, standing in the doorway, once more stealing the breath from her body.

"Ready?" he asked in that deep, sexy voice, the same whiskey-rough tone that melted her defenses and heated her blood.

Anytime.

Anyplace.

Anywhere.

Those words popped instantly into Emma's brain before she drew the veil of circumspection back down over them.

Be careful, she warned herself.

"Yes," she responded.

Chapter Six

It was comfortably warm in the Jeep as they sped through the cool Texas night.

Emma surreptitiously glanced at Burke as he drove. His left hand was steady on the wheel, his eyes focused straight ahead. Since entering the den, he'd been politeness personified, escorting her to the car, helping her inside. He'd been cool and distanced, as if he were performing a perfunctory service. Like a hired companion. Or, she thought, a careful watchdog, waiting for something untoward to happen.

Maybe she was letting her imagination get the best of her. He was probably being nice to his brother's girlfriend, no more, no less.

So why did she yearn for his attention? Or at least some small portion of his consideration?

Because she wanted to get to know him better. To see what made Burke Buchanan tick. To study him and discover the man beneath the tough outward shell. Whenever she painted a portrait, she always observed her subject for several days before starting. That way, she felt, the real person came through in her work.

Right now Emma wished that she'd tucked a small sketchbook into her purse. She had the urge to capture on paper the way Burke's short dark hair clung to his skull like a soft cap, the intense look he was capable of bestowing on a person, the shape of his long, slender fingers, the curve of his mobile mouth, the determined set of his shoulders.

"Are you comfortable?"

In the confines of the car, that bottomless voice wrapped around her with potent force. It was underscored by the classical guitar music coming from the Jeep's CD.

"Quite, thank you," she replied coolly, peeved that she hadn't the courage to push just a bit more and ask him to talk about himself. There was so much that she wanted to know, so much she was hungry to hear. But to do that now would risk alienating Burke, and she didn't want that. He was a man who wouldn't respond well to prying, regardless how innocent, and that's what she was afraid he would think she was doing.

Burke sliced a quick glance in her direction. "It's not much farther."

"Good," Emma replied, turning her head to gaze out the side window.

Was she getting bored in his company already? Burke wondered. She'd been sitting there in silence for most of the trip, as if she couldn't wait to get out of the car and be somewhere else, perhaps with someone else. Chances were she would find the place they were going too much a backwater for her cosmopolitan taste. No doubt she'd been to all the finest restaurants in Houston with Clay, places that oozed sophistication and expensive charm, unlike the roadhouse where they were meeting Vicky and Joe.

Maybe this hadn't been such a smart idea? He should have left well enough alone and declined Vicky's invitation.

No matter; it was too late now.

Burke turned off the highway into the crowded parking lot of an establishment that could best be described as having weathered a good number of years. A neon sign proudly proclaimed its name, Asa Harts.

Emma could tell this was a local place by the number of off-road vehicles, pickups, and motorcycles that clogged the lot. From the outside, it looked comfortable and inviting.

Swinging open her door, she stepped from the Jeep, enjoying the feel of the air as it brushed her face.

Her first impression was reinforced as they entered the roadhouse. A large English flatback clock bar of carved oak greeted her eyes as they adjusted to the dim lighting. High-backed booths, also carved of oak, were filled to capacity with patrons. Off to the side, she saw another room, smaller in size, which contained a minuscule dance floor and bandstand. A large, ornately designed Wurlizter jukebox held pride of place.

"Over here," called a feminine voice above the din of conversation and music.

"This way," Burke said, placing his arm about Emma's shoulders and guiding her past customers seated at the bar and waitresses carrying trays loaded with food and drink.

"Glad you both could make it," Vicky said warmly as the man beside her rose to greet the newcomers. "Joe, this is a special friend of Clay's, Emma Cantrell. Emma, this is Joe Crowne."

The man held out his hand and took Emma's. She smiled as she shook hands with him. He had the good looks of an actor, with his thick, dark blond hair pulled in a ponytail and a small, gold hoop earring adding to the overall package. It was obvious to Emma that Vicky was in love with him. Head over heels so. And, from the way that Joe looked at her when he resumed his seat, the feeling was mutual.

"Hope you weren't waiting long," Burke said as he slid into the booth after hanging up their jackets on the outside hooks, his muscled, jean-covered thigh just barely brushing Emma's.

"We got here about a half hour ago," Joe said, "so we're one beer ahead of you."

A waitress appeared at the booth as if by command. "Hi there," she said with a warm smile. "Anyone else having a drink here?"

Emma asked if they had the brand of beer that she preferred.

The waitress assured her that they did. "Honey, with all the Germans around here, myself included, we'd better have some German brands and more," she said, referring to the large community that had settled this particular part of Texas.

Burke ordered his usual, and helped himself to salsa and chips while they waited for their beers to come. "Did you order yet?" he asked his cousin.

"No, but I know what I want," Vicky said, taking a sip from her bottle, a light beer. "What I get every time I'm here, the venison steak." She chuckled, turning to Emma. "I'm such a creature of habit when I come here. They've got the best venison around. Marinated in port and cooked over a hickory-and-mesquite fire, then covered in a special sauce. Nothing can beat it.''

Burke picked up a plastic coated, double-sided menu that the waitress had left and handed it to Emma. ''You may want something else,'' he suggested, a touch of dryness in his tone.

''Yes, I think so,'' Emma said with a smile. ''My culinary tastes are a little less adventurous.''

''Do you cook a lot?'' Vicky asked.

''Pasta and salads mostly,'' Emma replied. ''Though I do like to make something special if I'm having friends over.''

''Hey, Vic,'' Joe said, teasing, ''that's more than you do, honey.''

Vicky poked him playfully in the ribs. ''That's because I'm smart and I let you do all the cooking,'' she rejoined. ''Besides, you didn't fall in love with me because I could cook.''

''Damn right,'' Joe said, nuzzling her ear.

Emma watched the easy interplay between the couple, envying them their happiness, their intimacy. This was how it should be between people who love each other, she thought. No hesitation, no barriers. Just open affection without fear, without effort. Joe had his arm around Vicky's shoulders, and they sat very close.

''Well, you won't have to worry about cooking if you don't want to, Emma,'' Vicky stated cheerfully. ''Clay's got a marvelous chef on staff, as I'm sure you know.''

''Yes, Mrs. Hudson is terrific,'' Emma agreed.

The waitress returned with their beers, and after setting them down, asked, ''You folks ready to order, or do you need more time?''

Seeing that Emma's beer came in a frosty-cold bottle instead of a mug, Burke spoke up. "I think that the lady would like a glass."

"Sorry, honey," the waitress said, leaning over to remove the bottle.

"The lady's okay, just as she is," Emma stated crisply. She proved it by downing a swallow from the bottle.

"I stand corrected," Burke said.

The waitress chuckled. "Honey, you got sass and gumption. I like that."

The four then placed their respective orders and the waitress went to deliver them to the cook.

Emma took a tortilla chip and loaded it with salsa, savoring the spicy taste. When she went to take another, her hand bumped into Burke's, and she pulled back instantly.

"Excuse me," she murmured.

"My fault," he replied.

"No, it was mine," Emma stated.

"Give me a break, you two," Vicky said with a laugh. "There's enough here for all of us." She and Joe demonstrated her point by both taking chips and dipping them into the salsa mixture.

Emma realized that she'd been making too much of the small incident. She felt foolish. It was just that the touch of Burke's hand set off a charge in her skin, like a connection with a live wire.

"Honey, I feel like dancing," Vicky said in a throaty voice. "Let's do it."

"Excuse us," Joe said as he slid out of the booth, Vicky in hand.

"I've got an idea," Vicky said to Joe. "Why don't you dance with Emma and I'll dance with my cousin?"

"That okay by you, Emma?" Joe inquired.

Feeling churlish should she refuse, Emma responded, "Sure, that's fine."

Burke stood up and took his cousin's hand as Joe took Emma's, and they walked into the adjoining room.

Vicky pulled some quarters from her tiny bag and slipped them into the jukebox.

A slow ballad filled the air as Emma went into Joe's arms. He held her close, but not too close. And she felt comfortable, like she was dancing with a relative or friend. Joe was a good dancer and she enjoyed the experience.

The rhythm abruptly changed as the next song came on. It was a sexy Latin melody, and Emma and Joe paused to watch the cousins move in time with the beat.

"Vicky's great, isn't she?" Joe asked.

Vicky, however, wasn't the principal focus of Emma's attention. Burke was.

She couldn't believe her eyes as she watched him dance. Here was a different Burke, another piece to the constantly changing puzzle. He was splendid. His lean, sinuous body moved rhythmically, swaying to the music. From her vantage point a few feet away, Emma could safely indulge in her fascination with him. There was a tamped passion in his movements, which conversely made her ache all the more. Unlike someone who danced nicely and in time, Burke seemed, to her eyes, to feel the music, becoming one with it. There was nothing mechanical or stiff about him. He was pure grace.

"See?" Vicky said, returning to Joe's side. "It's like riding a bicycle, Burke. You haven't forgotten a thing." To Emma she added, "He's really good, isn't he?"

Emma met Burke's brown eyes. They seemed to smolder. Or was it a reflection of her own heated temperature she saw there? "You are, you know," she said to him.

"Thanks," he replied offhandedly. "I had a good partner."

Vicky and Joe drifted off, caught up in their own needs as another song came on. It was an up-tempo number, intense in its lyrics, with a hard-driving two-step beat.

Burke held out his left hand.

Emma didn't hesitate. She accepted his offer.

Burke was playing with fire, and what's more, he knew it.

And what's more, he didn't give a good Texas damn.

Nothing was as important at that moment as answering the overwhelming urge to hold Emma in his arms. A dance gave him a valid excuse. She could refuse him if she wanted. It was her decision.

And she chose to accept his offer.

He pulled her gently against his body, shaping her curves to him. One hand held hers to his chest, the other slipped around her waist, his fingers splayed across her spine. The soft material of her teal blue sweater was smooth and warm to his touch. He wished he could feel her skin. It would, he knew, be the same.

Could she feel the reaction his body was having to the soft crush of her full breasts against his chest? To the inviting feel of her head as it rested upon his shoulder?

She must.

Long-suppressed desires flared to brilliant life in Burke's body as they moved in harmony. Like two interlocking pieces of a jigsaw, they fit perfectly.

Where was his usual detachment? His protective shell?

Shattered. Smashed. Ripped from him so skillfully he didn't know it was missing until he called upon it and found it gone.

Well, Burke acknowledged, he'd better get it back, fast. Before he made a mistake. Before he did something that couldn't be undone. Before he did the stupidest thing he could possibly do and fell in love with his brother's girlfriend.

Emma was reluctant to let go when the music ended, so natural did it seem to be held in Burke's strong arms, to listen to the steady beat of his heart beneath her ear. Why had she felt at home there? As if this was where she was supposed to be?

It just felt so right. The warmth from his body had seeped into hers, heating her, tightening her nipples, deepening the ache between her legs. An ache so exquisitely painful as to cross the line into bliss.

Emma flushed. What was happening to her? Where were these turbulent emotions coming from?

She'd danced with Clay—and other men—on numerous occasions, and nothing like this had ever occurred before. This was beyond the scope of her limited experience.

So why did Burke have to look so damned complacent now when she was churning up inside? It just wasn't fair.

"Coming?" he asked.

Emma snapped out of her musings and discovered that she and Burke were alone, Vicky and Joe having returned to the main room.

"Sorry," she said, "I was just thinking about something and got distracted."

"Clay?" he inquired, his tone low and slightly husky.

Would that was the case, Emma thought. It would certainly be far healthier for her peace of mind. "Yes," she lied. Better the safe fib than the perilous truth. "I was wondering what he was doing right now."

God, how adept with evasions she was becoming in so short a time. All because of feelings that confused her.

"More than likely he's thinking the same about you."

Emma shrugged her slim shoulders. "I doubt that. he's probably far too busy to have any free time to think about me." She hoped she was right. Guilt at her own reckless folly weighed heavily on her. Burke's ever increasing hold of her thoughts was a mental betrayal of Clay. But it was something she had no control over. Like sands washed by a powerful tide, Clay's image waned, replaced by that of Burke's.

"You can ask him yourself when he comes home tomorrow," Burke said. "He'll tell you different, I'm sure."

Their meals were waiting for them when they got back to the table. The waitress was pouring Vicky and Joe each a mug of hot coffee. "You two like any?" she asked, holding up the pot.

Since both Emma and Burke indicated that they did, the waitress, Patsy, went to get thick ironware mugs.

She came back in less than a minute and poured the dark brew, leaving a small bowl loaded with containers of cream. "Hope you enjoy it. And," she cautioned the group, "be sure and save some room for dessert. We got the best German chocolate cake in the state right here."

When Emma picked up the white mug, she noticed the design stenciled in black on the side. It was a single card from a deck: the ace of hearts.

Seeing her bemused expression, Burke commented. "Asa's brand of humor. A small joke for his customers."

"I think it's clever," Emma said, chuckling. "Do you think I could get one? It'd look great in my kitchen."

The sound of Emma's laughter was like a swift kick of adrenaline to Burke's system. "No problem," he said. "I'll see that you do."

She could tell that he was waiting, as if for an argument or protest that she could get it for herself.

Oh well, she could, but if she did, then it wouldn't be the same as having Burke get it for her. It would, Emma realized, make the mug just that more special. A souvenir of a day and night she wouldn't soon forget.

With a smile, she said, "Thanks. I'd appreciate that."

Emma hungrily attacked her chicken-fried steak, the generous home fries and the batter-dipped corn. Burke had ordered the same thing as Vicky and Joe, albeit a larger cut, a medium-rare venison steak and roasted potatoes.

"Do you want to try a piece?" Vicky asked.

"Go ahead," Joe urged. "I never thought I'd like it till Vicky insisted that I give it a try."

"Why not?" Emma answered, surprising even herself. "I'm game."

Vicky and Joe laughed at the weak pun, as did Emma.

Burke sliced a small portion for her from his own steak. Instead of putting it on her plate so that she could help herself, he held out his fork.

Emma wet her lips. She'd never eaten from someone else's utensil before. It seemed so intimate a gesture.

Slowly she leaned forward and took the meat Burke held out for her, chewing it carefully.

"Well?" It was Vicky who spoke, and yet Emma couldn't take her eyes from Burke's face as he waited for her verdict.

"Good," she declared. "Really good." She wet her lips again, enjoying the taste.

Burke smiled, then cut another piece for himself, lifting the fork to his own mouth.

Emma watched him eat it before she forced herself to go back to her own meal. "The sauce is wonderful."

"Family recipe of the Harts," Vicky commented. "Peppercorns and port."

"Very simple," Emma stated.

Simple?

No way. Everything was getting more and more complicated by the minute. Blinders were being lifted. Chinks in the armor were being discovered.

"What about dessert at our house?" Vicky asked. "We don't live far from here."

Emma turned her head and looked at Burke.

He considered for a moment. "Okay," he eventually replied.

"Great," Vicky announced. "I think I'll make it real easy and see if I can negotiate for one of their cakes. *Dios,* I can taste it already. Scoot, sweetie," she said to Joe.

"Please," Emma offered, reaching for her own purse. "Let me."

"Nonsense," Vicky stated as she stood up. "You're a guest, Emma. Relax and enjoy our brand of Texas hospitality."

Emma murmured a thank-you in response.

Within twenty-five minutes they were on their way to the house Vicky shared with Joe outside the town of Derran, founded, Emma discovered, by one of Burke's

ancestors. She was almost overwhelmed by the importance of this family in Texas history. It was a legacy she
envied.

It was then that the idea for a new painting came to
her. She even knew the title: *Texas Pride*. Tomorrow she
would ask Santina if there were any paintings or photographs of the original owners that she could look at,
and then she would make a few preliminary sketches.
She saw the composition of the picture clearly, a blend
of the past and present. And at its heart, she saw Burke.

Vicky and Joe had made the journey on Joe's Harley,
and were able to slip out of the parking lot as soon as the
two couples left the roadhouse. When Burke and Emma
pulled up at the home minutes after them, the lights were
already on.

Emma thought it a lovely place. A renovated Victorian with a charming wraparound porch, it looked solid
and welcoming.

Burke glanced up at the sky as they walked up the low,
wide stone steps. "Snow's coming," he said.

Tubs containing blends of small cacti were scattered
on the painted porch floor. Emma recognized several
varieties from her own collection, held in earthenware
pots that decorated her studio and her house.

Vicky stood in the doorway. "Welcome."

She took their coats and hung them on a brass tree in
the hallway. "Joe's lighting a fire in the living room. I
think he mentioned challenging you to a game of pool,
Burke."

"Okay by me," he said, heading up the polished
staircase to the second floor. Seconds later, Joe followed.

"Emma, come help me with the coffee, if you don't mind," Vicky requested, walking down the narrow hallway.

"Gladly," Emma answered, following her into a brightly light kitchen with sunny apricot walls.

"There's a cake plate in the cabinet over there," Vicky said, pointing to the spot while she scooped fresh coffee into the filtered basket and added cold water to the pot. "Sorry, I only have regular," she added. "We don't drink decaf."

"That's fine by me, since that's what I prefer, anyway," Emma responded as she located the large cut-glass dish and lid. She brought it down and opened up the box that the cake was in, carefully removing it and placing it on the glass. "Do you have a cake server?"

Vicky opened a drawer and took out an antique silver piece, handing it to Emma. Then she got out four dessert plates.

"What a lovely china pattern," Emma murmured.

"They're heirlooms, from my—and Burke's—grandmother Rayburne. She gave them to me on my twenty-first birthday. She called it a hope-chest gift. A not-so-subtle hint that I should get married."

Emma gazed at one of the small china plates. In the center was a bouquet of deep yellow roses; the border was decorated with tiny yellow rosebuds. As an artist, she responded to the beauty of the piece.

"I'm so glad that we had this chance to get to know each other better," Vicky said, taking out matching cups and saucers, along with creamer and sugar bowl. "I'm only sorry that Clay couldn't have been here. But in a funny way, I'm actually glad that he isn't," she confessed.

"Why?"

"Because then Burke wouldn't have come," she stated. "I just about have to threaten him to get him to come here as it is." Vicky added napkins to the tray she was preparing. "He devotes so much of his energy to the ranch, and he does so little for himself. In terms of personal time, I mean. It's been ages since he's been out and had fun."

"Really?" Emma would have thought that Burke, a handsome, single, rich man, would have had his pick of women.

"Yes," Vicky confided as she cut generous slices of the cake, swiping one index finger along the thick edge of chocolate frosting that circled the bottom of the cake and tasting it. "Sorry, never could resist.... Where was I? Oh yes, Burke." She sat down at the round oak table and invited Emma to do the same. "I think I'm a fairly good judge of character, and I think what I have to say will be kept confidential, won't it?"

Emma was surprised by the other woman's words, by the trust Vicky was placing in her. "Yes, it will," she hastily assured her.

"Good. I just knew my intuition was right. You've met Jessie, Burke's daughter, haven't you?"

Emma grinned. "Yes. She seems a delightful little girl."

"No thanks to Burke's ex-wife," Vicky said bitterly. "It's been all Burke's doing that Jessie is as well adjusted as she is. Of course, my aunt and uncle help, and so do Clay and Drew when they can, but it was Burke who raised his daughter since the day she was born, Burke who changed diapers, Burke who rearranged his life so that his daughter would come first. He was a boy when he first got married, Emma. Only seventeen. But he knew the meaning of the words *do the right thing*."

Vicky let out a sigh. "He's put all his energy into the ranch and into seeing that Jessie is taken care of properly. That leaves little time for an ordinary social life."

"But surely he's dated?"

"Not to my knowledge," Vicky declared, "and we're close. More like brother and sister, since our birthdays are only a few weeks apart."

Emma said softly, "I sensed that you and Burke had a special bond."

"We do," Vicky agreed. "And that's why I wish he could find someone as nice as you to care about him. Someone to erase all the hateful things that rotten bitch—I'm sorry but there's no other word to describe her—did to him. She messed with his mind, putting him through an emotional wringer."

"Clay's mentioned her, and he feels the same, I know."

"He should," Vicky insisted. "You know why? Celia tried to drive a wedge between him and his brother when she was married to Burke. She told Burke that Clay had tried numerous times to come on to her."

Emma immediately defended her boyfriend. "Clay wouldn't do that."

"That's right," Vicky agreed. "And Burke knew it. He and Clay are too close for that to have ever happened, especially when Celia was pregnant with Jessie. She thought that she could pull her tricks and the men would fall in with her plan. It backfired."

"Does Burke have sole custody of Jessie?"

"Yes, thank God. Could you imagine the kind of life Jessie would be exposed to if she had to live with her mother? It makes me ill just to think about it. Burke made sure when he divorced Celia that she wouldn't ever be a part of Jessie's life."

"How did he do that?" Emma knew she shouldn't pry any further, but she couldn't pretend she wasn't interested.

"By making it worth her while. Simple as that."

"You mean she willingly took money to stay out of her child's life?"

"Exactly. A very large sum."

Emma was chagrined. "How could she do that? Jessie's such a lovely girl."

"Money talks," Vicky answered bluntly. "It's all Celia was ever interested in from Burke—the Buchanan name and a share of the Buchanan fortune."

Emma felt a measure of sadness sweep over her. How hurt Burke must have felt to have been seen as only a means to a monetary end. Used and discarded when he no longer served a purpose. And at such a young age. That had to have colored his views on love and trust. It also explained his rather cool initial reception of her; he must be wondering if she was after Clay for the same reason.

"Emma?"

She blinked. "Sorry."

"So now you can see why I was so happy that Burke came out with us this evening, even if it was only to escort his brother's girlfriend. It's a beginning, I hope. Maybe he'll finally accept the invitations I keep tossing his way to meet some of my friends."

Had Burke loved Celia? Emma wondered. Is that why he'd married her? She asked that question out loud.

"Gracious no," Vicky insisted with a shake of her head. "Burke did what was right by his child. He made a man's decision—to take responsibility for a life he helped create. For him, that meant marriage. All Celia wanted was a pampered, jet-set lifestyle and she thought her pregnancy would be the ticket. When she discovered she wasn't going to have that lifestyle, she decided to bail out. She whined and pleaded, but it didn't get her anywhere. So she started messing with his head. Celia could be very cruel and spiteful when she wanted to be. In the end, she got the one thing she loved more than anything else—money. And Burke got his freedom and his daughter. Fair trade."

"Thank God! It sounds like he and Jessie are well rid of her," Emma exclaimed. She realized that it hurt to think of Burke suffering, even if it was in the past.

Or was it?

He must still carry the scars from his brief marriage. How could he not?

It explained so much.

"Would you bring in the coffee while I get this tray?" Vicky asked, pulling Emma from her thoughts and back to the present.

"Sure." She stood and picked up the pot, emptying it into the insulated coffee urn that Vicky had already provided.

"And you will keep this between us?"

Emma nodded.

"Good. Now, let's go see if we can interest the men in some dessert."

Chapter Seven

Burke was right.

When they left Vicky's house a little after ten, the snow had just begun. It was a soft, light snowfall, dusting the roads and trees, washing everything with a white tint, giving this section of the Texas Hill Country a fairy-tale appearance.

All the way to the ranch, warmly cocooned in the Jeep, Emma found her thoughts wandering back to the hours just past, to the things she'd learned about Burke from Vicky, things that tugged at Emma's heart.

She wanted to reach out and touch him in some way. To let him know that she cared, that she was there if he needed someone to talk to.

But she couldn't say anything. To do so would be to betray Vicky's confidence, and her own vulnerability toward him. And she was vulnerable. More so with this man than any she'd ever met before. Not even Clay, the man she was considering spending her life with, had this power to make her want to offer comfort and support without limit, to give and give until the hurt vanished.

That thought frightened her.

Emma was in dangerous territory, coming closer and closer to the point of no return.

As they pulled into the long drive leading to the main house, she grew increasingly restless. She didn't want to go directly inside and straight upstairs. She wanted to linger awhile longer. She wanted to stop time and hold it captive in her hands. She wanted to savor the beauty and magic of this night.

Right now she probably wanted too damn much.

When Burke stopped the car near the front entrance, Emma murmured, "I don't want to go in just yet."

He put the car in park and turned slightly in his seat, focusing his gaze on her. "You don't?"

"No," she replied, glad that he couldn't see her face clearly just then. "If you don't mind, I'd like to take a walk."

"A walk?" Burke asked, one brow raised. "In case you hadn't noticed, it's snowing."

"Haven't you ever taken a walk in the snow?"

"Not unless I had to," he responded.

"Then you should." Emma unfastened her seat belt and opened the door, shutting it as quietly as she could. Before Burke could object, she was walking in the direction of the paddock fence.

She heard the car pull away toward the large, multi-vehicle garage that housed the various Buchanan cars, forcing herself to keep focused on the area ahead of her and not on the man behind.

Some minutes later Burke found Emma standing near the paddock looking out into the lightly falling snow.

She was easy to spot, with the gray skies overhead reflecting every bit of natural light. She leaned on the fence, obviously focused on something. Snow dusted her dark curls. Her breath hung in the air in puffs.

If only...

If only what? Burke asked himself.

If only she wasn't his brother's girlfriend? If only he'd met her first? If only she was free of the future and he was free of the past?

He scowled. Damn it, anyway.

He was reluctant to go inside and leave her to fend for herself. True, she was safe, but he couldn't go in and pretend that he didn't want to be with her when he did.

"What are you thinking?" It was the second time tonight he'd asked her that. She was liable to believe his conversational skills were sadly lacking. But the truth was he *did* want to know what she was thinking. More so with each minute he spent in her company.

Emma turned her head when she heard his voice. "Actually," she said softly, "I was seeing your horse out there, prancing in the snow."

"Really?" Burke sounded skeptical.

Emma laughed. "Yes, really. *Compañero* is a magnificent animal. Think how he'd look with a backdrop of snow-covered trees, that rocky creek we visited today in the foreground to one side, steam blowing from his nostrils as he pauses to survey the land he's king of."

"You can see all that?"

She tapped her forehead with a gloved finger. "It's all in here."

He joined her at the fence. "That's quite a special gift you have."

"A compliment, Mr. Buchanan?"

When he didn't respond, Emma turned completely around so that she was facing him. She had the most beautiful eyes, he thought. Such an unusual color, surrounded by thick dark lashes. And her cheeks. They were flushed from the cold.

Burke pulled off his suede glove and reached out his left hand. He stroked his fingertips along the line of her face, from her temple to her jaw, marveling at how soft her skin was. Even softer than he'd imagined.

Her own gloved hand reached out and casually brushed a few flakes of snow from his forehead.

Abruptly, Burke withdrew his hand and took a step back, replacing the glove. His voice was gruff. "We'd better be getting inside."

"Yes," Emma said, dropping her lashes. "I suppose we should." She regretted giving in to the impulse to touch him. She shouldn't have. In doing that, she felt she'd somehow crossed an invisible line. But she'd only been reacting to the warm feel of his own fingers on her skin.

They made the short journey in silence, and as they reached the door, pausing beneath the light in the entranceway, Burke heard himself make a request that came spontaneously from within.

"Would you like something to drink?"

"A nightcap?"

He shrugged. "Whatever."

"Yes, I would." Her voice was low, barely above a whisper. She raised one hand to her damp curls. "Just let me give my hair a quick once-over with a towel and I'll be right back."

"Meet me in the den," Burke instructed. He watched as Emma crept up the stairs, shoes in hand. He waited until she disappeared from view before he walked down the hallway and into the den. Shucking off his jacket, he tossed it onto the leather chair, then made his way over to the fireplace and hunkered down. Adding a small log to the dying embers, he successfully rebuilt the fire into a warming glow. He tossed in several apple chips from a brass canister to add a distinctive scent to the flames.

That accomplished, Burke stood up, setting in place the protective glass screen. He really was loco, inviting her for a late-night drink. What the hell had he been thinking?

Problem was, he wasn't thinking. He was reacting. Allowing his emotions, his needs, to overcome his common sense.

Burke stepped over to the built-in cabinet next to the fireplace and retrieved a bottle of brandy. Not just any old brand, but a rare vintage. His father's favorite. Clay's favorite, also.

Pouring equal amounts into two distinctive Waterford crystal snifters, Burke picked up one glass, held it in his palms and rolled it back and forth between his hands. He took a sip, letting the brandy slide down his throat and warm his insides.

He could berate himself as much as he wished, but he still wouldn't change his mind. He was determined to hold on to whatever time he could steal with her.

Stolen moments.

He was in danger of becoming melodramatic, he warned himself. Yet Burke didn't really care. He pushed aside the self-censure, the guilt, finding it all too difficult to bring this evening to its inevitable conclusion. Clay would be back at the ranch well before they sat down to the combined birthday-Thanksgiving dinner tomorrow. Then Burke would fade out of the picture and let Clay and Emma get on with their lives.

He took another swallow of the brandy. But could he, truly?

Emma sat on her bed, towel in hand. She'd removed the minimal amount of moisture from her hair. What she was doing now was stalling, avoiding the decision she had to make. Should she go back downstairs and join Burke for that drink? Just contemplating it sent her heart rate pounding.

Or should she stay where she was? Make up some excuse in the morning that she'd been too tired and had fallen asleep? Which was plausible. It had been a very long day, with lots of activities crammed into it.

She knew what she wanted to do.

She knew what she ought to do.

Emma stood up and returned the towel to the rack in the bathroom. She was going to share that drink with him. After all, it would be rude to simply leave him waiting for her.

Rude had nothing to do with it.

She *wanted* to go back downstairs and share the time alone with him. Having a drink was only an excuse. Thin, perhaps, but still valid.

Emma had removed her damp shoes before coming upstairs, so, creeping along like a well-trained thief, she padded down the darkened hallway in her thick socks, careful not to make any noise that might waken the household.

Burke was standing by the stone fireplace, one hand casually resting on the low mantel, the other cradling a snifter of amber liquid, when she entered. There was one lamp lit in the room, an antique Victorian piece. It provided a low light, keeping the room rather intimate. The only other illumination was from the flames of the fire.

Emma thought the mood soft, seductive. Or was that only her wishful imagination?

Burke lifted his head as she closed the pocket doors behind her, sealing them off from the hall. She walked slowly across the carpet, taking the drink he offered her.

Emma sipped at it, enjoying the taste. She recognized the brand, but refrained from commenting, reluctant to drag Clay's name into this quiet time. Instead, she savored the shared solitude, thankful for the moment. Burke looked contemplative and terribly handsome.

"I had a good time with Vicky and Joe tonight," she said, taking a seat on the couch, her legs curled up under her. Her eyes made a slow inventory of Burke's tall body as he poured himself a small measure more of the brandy. He was made to wear jeans, she thought. And the hunter green, thin wale corduroy shirt defined his lean torso and showed off his golden skin to perfection.

"They're good people," Burke asserted, joining her on the couch.

"I thought it was so interesting how they met," Emma said. "Imagine, walking into a shop and discovering not only a master artisan, but the man of your dreams." Emma took another small sip of her drink. She refused to add that it seemed so romantic, so destined, to be on one path and find the road held another, albeit unexpected, traveler who was going in the same direction. How fascinating the opportunity, how amazing the surprise.

"Joe's good to her and good for her," Burke commented.

Emma stretched one arm along the back of the couch, her fingers absently caressing the upholstery material. "You're very protective of Vicky, aren't you?"

Burke didn't answer the question right away. He took a drink, relishing the potent taste of the brandy, aware of her hand sliding across the fabric of the couch. He was becoming more aroused by the second. "I'm protective of all my family," he admitted.

Emma found that an intriguing prospect. Burke was the kind of man who saw protection as an old-fashioned virtue. For him, it was a natural consequence of his upbringing and his heritage. Raised with a tradition of strength and responsibility, a man of his ilk could do no less. And for him, she thought, protection would involve caring, not confining. It would mean being the wind beneath one's wings, never the fetters.

What would it feel like to be in that position? Strange, she would assume. Emma had been on her own for so long, relying on herself. This was a man for whom family came first. Yet she still sensed that he was in some way a man alone. A man tied to a path that was well worn and comfortable, though not necessarily the best option for him.

It would take a special woman to lure Burke from his solitary course. A woman who could make him forget the hurts of the past and concentrate instead on what the future might hold. A woman without lies or traps.

"And what are you protective of?" Burke asked.

Emma looked into his coffee brown eyes and felt herself sinking into their depths. Burke's eyes were more potent than the brandy, for they reached into her soul, intoxicating her with the secrets they held.

Emma blinked. "Myself, I suppose."

"How so?"

"I'm careful."

"Careful?" he inquired quizzically. "About what?"

"People. Things. My work."

"Give me an example." Burke's curiosity was fired. Did she keep for her art alone the passion that was so visible in her work?

"I weigh things in my head. You know, consider all the options. Think things through," she disclosed. "I don't rush into anything blindly. Options have to make sense to me."

"And what about people?"

"Normally, I don't jump into relationships," she confessed. "I like to take things slow and easy."

Taking things slow and easy brought up all sorts of pictures in Burke's mind. His hand slowly skimming her naked breasts, circling and cupping, his mouth leisurely mating with hers, deep and sweet. His body thrusting into her lush form, slow and easy, prolonging the inevitable conclusion until they both burst from the beauty of it.

Damn! It was getting way too hot in the room. What he needed was a slap of something cold to cool his ardor. Like a long walk in the snow.

"Work?" he managed to ask, barely controlling the hunger in his voice.

"I won't exploit my gift, or paint something just because it's in," she stated. "Art is not just how I make my living, it's who I am. That makes me protective of what I do and where I do it. And to what causes I lend my support."

"I know what you mean," Burke said with a touch of cynicism. "People are always after the Buchanan name for what it can do for them, for how it can be used or exploited. It's a hard lesson to learn, but it forces you to take stock and develop your instincts."

Right now Burke fought the instincts that demanded he reach out and draw Emma to him, that he indulge in kissing her until they were both demanding more.

Emma couldn't help it; she yawned. "I'm sorry."

"Don't apologize," Burke insisted, putting down his own snifter and taking the half-filled glass from her hand. "It has been a long day, after all. Go to bed."

The next words slipped out of Emma's mouth before she could recall them. "Are you coming?"

Burke looked at her. He longed to ask if that was an invitation.

And what if it had been? What would he do?

Nothing.

But God, how much he wanted to kiss her right now, to feel the touch of that silky smooth skin again.

Emma blushed. Damn! It sounded like she was issuing Burke an invitation to join her upstairs. She hoped that he realized she wasn't. At least not really. Perhaps her subconscious was acting up, playing out the fantasy.

"I think I'll be up in a little while," he responded in a low tone.

Emma stood. "Good night then."

Burke waited for her to leave the room before he expelled the breath that threatened to constrict his chest. How much he wanted to follow her up those stairs and pull her into his own room. Or any room, for that matter, as long as it contained a bed. Actually, that wasn't quite true. He wanted a room that guaranteed them privacy; that was the only requirement.

What the hell was he going to do with the situation he found himself in?

Nothing, for now. What could he do?

* * *

Emma curled under the down comforter, snuggling into the warmth, a kittenish smile curving her full lips. She was in that realm of being half asleep, half awake, when dreams and reality blended into one. She hugged the pillow to her, sighing deeply. It had been so good, so wonderful. A dark, mysterious man had skillfully seduced her, whispering powerful words inviting surrender while his slow hands roamed her body, stroking, caressing, feathering, provoking. He was sure and adept, arousing her to a growing state of ecstasy. He knew the meaning of taking his time, of building the moment. She wanted to see his face, to discover who this man was who could produce such feelings within her, but he remained elusive, his face hidden by shadows. Only his deep, husky voice—guiding her, soothing her, instructing her—seemed familiar, yet for some reason she couldn't remember a name, couldn't even whisper it in wonder. To do so would break the spell, and she couldn't risk that. All that mattered was this feeling of completeness, of being one with this dark stranger.

From somewhere else came the sound of a buzz, ringing steadily. It eventually overpowered and drowned out the man's voice, pushing the dream into thin air.

Emma lifted her head and saw the blinking light of her bedside telephone. Momentarily disoriented, she turned her head, as if expecting to see someone there, sharing the bed with her. It had all seemed so real.

But it wasn't. It had been her overactive imagination taking her on a dark journey into midnight fantasies and beyond.

"Hello," she muttered, picking up the receiver, her voice still husky from sleep.

"There's a call for you on line one," Santina said. "It's Clay."

"Thank you," Emma murmured groggily, pressing the flashing button on the phone.

"Hello, darling," Clay said.

His voice was a splash of cold water on her heated thoughts.

"Where are you?" She tried to focus on the small clock at her bedside. It read 9:32 a.m.

"Unfortunately," he explained, "I'm still in San Francisco."

"You are coming back today, aren't you?"

Clay cleared his throat. "I'm afraid I can't. This project is going to take more time than I first thought, and I've got to see it through."

"I understand." And she did. Clay was CEO of a large financial organization that demanded a good deal of his time and energy. She knew he thrived on its daily challenges. He'd been very up-front about that when they first began to date. Her own work drove her as well, so she easily understood where Clay was coming from. But a niggling doubt suddenly arose: had this been a convenient safety net for her, because she knew there was something else Clay cared for as much or more than her? Something he could fall back on if he needed to?

"Emma. Are you there?" His solid, pleasant voice drew her back to the conversation. "Don't be sweet. Scream if you want," he said. "I know that I'm angry. This wasn't how I planned on spending my Thanksgiving. Damn it," he murmured softly. "I wanted to spend it with you, not with pages upon pages of financial data." A long, drawn-out sigh came over the line. "I'm sorry, sweetheart, really I am."

"I know you are," Emma conceded. "It couldn't be helped."

"I'm a lucky man to have you in my life," he stated. "You know that?"

Emma clenched the receiver. "I hope you'll always feel like that, Clay."

"Honey, I can't imagine why I wouldn't," he assured her.

"So, do you have any idea when you'll get back to the ranch?" she asked, maintaining a neutral tone.

"No, unfortunately, I don't," he replied. "It depends on how soon we can wrap up the problems with this deal. I want to make sure all the conditions I wanted in the first place are met so that we can begin construction as soon as possible. I won't compromise with what I want."

Emma admired that about him—he had integrity. A trait he shared with his younger brother.

Burke.

Oh my God! she thought with a shock. It'd been his voice in the dream. It all came flooding back to her with a clarity that hurt.

"So why don't you continue on as we'd planned? Stay the rest of the weekend and get to know everyone there. I'll keep you posted on the situation here, let you know the instant I can get away."

"I have to leave by Monday morning," she reminded him. "Remember I need to be in New York by the end of next week, and I want to get back to my own house for a few days."

"If I'm not at the ranch by Sunday evening, I'll make sure my pilot is there to fly you back to New Mexico, I promise."

"You don't have to do that, Clay."

He laughed. "I know I don't, sweetheart. I want to." A female voice in the background called his name. "Look, I have to go. Linda's waving a sheaf of computer paper at me and we have an early breakfast meeting. So much for a holiday." He lowered his voice so that she alone would hear him. "I miss you, you know."

Emma smoothed her tongue across her lips. "I miss you, too, Clay."

"I'll try and call back later tonight," he promised. "I've already explained to Mama that I won't be there. Give Jessie a birthday hug and kiss for me, would you?"

"Of course," she promised, telling him goodbye. She hung up the phone. Clay wasn't coming back, and she was stuck here. But she was sure she could make up some excuse and get someone from the ranch to drive her into San Antonio, where she could catch a plane home or rent a car. She would make it through his family dinner and then leave with a clear conscience. There was nothing holding her here.

Liar. Nothing except a dawning truth she wasn't willing to face.

A determined rap sounded on her door.

"Come in," Emma said.

Santina Buchanan entered, bearing a breakfast tray.

"You didn't have to do this," Emma protested gently as she sat up in bed.

"I know I didn't," Santina said, placing the tray upon the ivy green comforter. "I wanted to. After all, you're a guest here, and we like to spoil our guests whenever possible. So sit back and enjoy."

"How could I not?" Emma asked, lifting the lid from a plate and discovering crisp slices of bacon and wedges of fresh fruit. A white, wicker basket held two plump honey-wheat muffins and a tiny jam pot containing thick orange marmalade. A small carafe of hot coffee, along with sugar and cream, completed the repast. "This looks great," Emma said, realizing that she was hungry.

Santina took a seat in the nearby chair. "Did you have a good time last night?" she asked.

Emma wondered for a minute how she should answer. After all, this woman was Clay's mother, too. Would she sound disloyal if she said that she'd had a great time?

"Wonderful, in fact," Emma replied honestly. "I really like both Vicky and Joe."

Santina nodded her head and smiled. "I'm glad. I know Burke enjoyed himself, as well."

Emma stared at her, her eyes wide with curiosity. "He did?"

"Yes," Santina answered. "Before he rode out this morning with Jessie, he told me about last night."

But not all of it, Emma suspected. How would his mother react if she knew that Burke and Emma had shared even more time together over a drink downstairs? Alone, while everyone else was asleep? Would Santina think her a willful, capricious flirt, who, if one brother wasn't available, latched on to the other? How could Emma explain that she was drawn to Burke in ways she hadn't believed possible? Ways that frightened her with the depth of sensation they evoked?

She couldn't confide in Santina, so she kept her thoughts to herself.

"It's so rare Burke goes out that I'm pleased he had someone to share his evening with."

Emma decided that it was time to change the topic before Santina detected something. The woman was sharp and very intuitive. Emma didn't want to arouse any untoward suspicions, especially since she really liked her hostess and very much wanted the feeling to be mutual.

"Do you by any chance have any old photographs of your family that I could see?" she asked.

Santina nodded. "Yes, as a matter of fact, I do. There are plenty of photo albums that I could lend you if you'd like." Good manners kept her from commenting on her guest's sudden and surprising request.

"I'd really appreciate that, if you wouldn't mind," Emma said, selecting one of the muffins.

"It's no bother, my dear," Santina responded in a warm tone. "Are you looking for anyone in particular?"

"Actually, yes. I'd like to see anything on the original Buchanans, if you have it. Burke talked about them yesterday, and they seemed fascinating."

"Oh, indeed they were, and yes, we do have some photos of them." Santina rose gracefully. "There's a portrait in Burke's office that was painted on their silver wedding anniversary. It is simply beautiful. You should have him show it to you. As an artist, you'll like it, I'm sure. I'll go see about the photographs right away," she added. "Lunch will be light today, as we have our Thanksgiving dinner around four."

By the time Emma had washed and dressed, Santina had delivered several thick, leather albums to her room. They were crammed with pictures of men and women who seemed to exude pride and strength, courage and determination. There were several people Emma would like to have met.

The last album had a Post-It note on the cover: "I know this is not what you wanted, but I couldn't resist. Enjoy!"

Emma flipped it open and discovered it contained photos of Clay, Burke and another boy she assumed was Drew. From baby photos to more formal snapshots, from everyday life around the ranch to high-school sports and social gatherings, their growing-up years were documented.

She thumbed through the pages slowly until she came to one photograph that stopped her.

It was of Burke, taken just after the birth of his daughter. His hair was longer, brushing his shoulders in thick strands. He cradled Jessie in his arms, smiling proudly into the lens of the camera.

Emma touched the photo reverently with her fingertips. There was so much emotion contained in that one picture. What a pity, she thought, that he hadn't had other children on which to lavish his love and care. There was a softness about him in this shot that made her heart break.

He was the kind of man who would walk through fire for anyone he loved; it was all there in his face. He was decent, stubborn, occasionally brooding and proud.

Tears rolled down her cheeks. Emma blinked and wiped them away with the back of her hand.

She loved him.

Chapter Eight

She loved Burke.

Emma finally had the answer she'd sought since that first night. This feeling had taken root—so deep and so true that to deny it would be foolish. It was part of her now, soul deep, leaving room in her heart for no other man.

Now what was she going to do about it?

Emma sat down, the photo album gripped tightly in her hands, her mind still reeling from the shock of what she'd just admitted to herself.

She was in love with Burke Buchanan, the brother of the man she'd been dating and had even considered marrying.

Emma stared at the photo of Burke and Jessie again. In her vivid imagination, she could envision another photograph: Burke older, cradling another baby in his arms; Jessie standing proudly beside him. The look on

his face was one of pure, unadulterated happiness. It was
there in the way he smiled, the very same smile that
warmed her heart.

Oh God, what was she going to do?

She shut the leather album and placed it on the floor.
Maybe, just maybe, she was wrong. Maybe she didn't
love him.

A deep wave of sadness washed over Emma. The
thought of never seeing Burke again, of never being in
his company, of never hearing that tempting voice, was
too dismal to contemplate. Within days he'd become an
integral part of her life. To remove him from it would rip
the fabric of her existence, so closely interwoven had
they become.

Yet what choice did she have, really? Burke saw her
only as the woman his older brother wanted to marry. To
him she was a stranger, an outsider. She couldn't very
well run up to him, declaring her newfound, undying
love. Emma could well imagine Burke's reaction were
she to do something so foolish and forward. Scorn
would appear in his cool brown eyes, in the slight flaring of his nostrils, in the sardonic curl of his mouth—a
ready condemnation for her rejection of his brother. It
would be to him, she was sure, another example of the
betrayal of a woman. Give your heart and have it handed
back to you in pieces, along with your pride.

Coldness crept over her skin. How was she going to
endure the next few days? She hadn't seen Burke since
late last night, and already her heart ached to catch a
glimpse of him.

What was she going to say to Clay? How could she
reasonably explain to him that there was no way she
could consent to wed him now? How did you tell someone who presumably loved you that you realized you

didn't feel the same? That somehow you had fallen in love with another man, and that, ironically, the other man was his own younger brother—a man he loved, respected and trusted?

Emma understood that to admit the truth to Clay would be to drive a wedge between the brothers. She cared too much for Clay to ever want to deliberately hurt him. Discovering that she was turning down his proposal because she now loved his brother would be like pouring salt into whatever wounds he sustained from their breakup.

Emma wrapped her arms about herself, her head bent as she thought about the situation. It was all so complicated. So damnably complicated. To finally recognize love, and then be forced to turn her back on it before she could discover if there was any chance for happiness, was a bitter pill to swallow.

It wasn't fair.

But then, Emma realized, nothing about this situation was fair. Hurt was inevitable. She accepted it for herself, and realized that in doing so, she would hurt Clay. If only she could wave a magic wand and wipe away all traces of pain from what she had to do.

The thought that whatever hurt she would inflict would be lessened by lying about her motives eased her guilt, however marginally. Clay would be spared the pain of the absolute truth. She owed him that, because she did love him—though she understood now it was the love of a good friend, or the love of a brother. A bond existed between them, there was no denying that fact. But it wasn't the kind of bond Clay wanted with her.

In shielding Clay from the real truth, she would also be protecting Burke, by preserving his relationship with his brother. Their closeness was enviable. She couldn't be the one to destroy it.

What did her future hold now? The certainty of pain and loneliness as companions.

With a surprising clarity, Emma knew she'd never love another man as completely as she loved Burke Buchanan. This was the love she'd waited for her whole life—and now she couldn't claim it. This was the man for whom she'd subconsciously been saving her complete passion—and now she would never experience it.

The idea of discovering all the delights of lovemaking in Burke's arms was a bittersweet thought that made Emma ache all the more. What would it have been like to experience physical union with him? What kind of lover would he have been if he'd loved her as deeply as she loved him?

Her mind spun off into images that provoked and excited, mental pictures that delighted and challenged, touching her in ways that tantalized, comforted and haunted. Heat flushed Emma's body as she envisioned the two of them in her big bed, their bodies intertwined, sunlight streaming through the many windows.

It was such a compelling fantasy.

However, that's all it ever could be.

Emma picked up the album once again. She couldn't resist another look at the photographs. Scanning the pages, she stopped to stare at a few in the collection. Once again she found herself drawn to the younger Burke, to the promise and the sorrow in his eyes. If only she'd known him then, maybe she could have helped ease the pain his selfish wife had inflicted upon him.

God knows she would love to give it a try even now, years later.

Maybe some things were never meant to be, she thought. No matter how much one wanted them.

Then why did it hurt so much?

As he rode his horse over the snow-covered range, Burke thought about the scene Emma had described to him last night, the one she wanted to paint. Thinking about that led him along a dangerous path as he recalled the time they'd spent together afterward. As if he had a VCR in his mind, each moment was rewound and played back in his head. What was it he'd seen in her eyes? What message could he extract from the way she'd moved, the way she'd talked? What was it about this woman that urged him to trust her?

Damn it! She was burrowing under his defenses, apparently without even trying. Her very presence was disturbing his equilibrium, his carefully controlled desire, the very rules he lived by.

What was he going to do when she married his brother? Burke assumed it was a certainty and why not? Clay was smart, successful, rich and handsome, the type of man who knew his way around the boardroom and the bedroom. Clay was the kind of man women wanted, the kind of man women fell in love with. Unlike himself, Clay carried no emotional baggage, which was a definite plus to a woman. Why wouldn't Emma want to marry him?

Hell, her saying yes was inevitable, Burke acknowledged sourly. And when that happened, how was he to handle Emma as a part of his family? As a sister?

He'd make do. He'd have to. Thankfully, Clay and Emma would live elsewhere, their time at the ranch almost nonexistent. He would endure their occasional visits as best he could. In time, things would change.

Feelings would blur, passions would abate. Burke had to believe that or he would go mad from wanting the impossible.

He still couldn't believe this had all happened so quickly. Only days ago she'd been an enigma, a question mark waiting to be explored. Now she was a woman he wanted with a hot, burning hunger he'd never experienced before.

"Daddy, watch me!" Jessie shouted as she took her horse over a stone jump.

His thoughts interrupted, Burke turned his attention to his daughter as she skillfully handled the jump, she and her mount leaping over the obstacle with ease. He clapped his gloved hands together, indicating his approval.

Jessie rode over to where her father sat atop his horse. "We should have asked Emma to come with us," she stated.

As if on cue, Renegade barked his two cents' worth.

"See? Even Renegade thinks so," the girl said.

Burke raised his brows skeptically at his daughter's remark. "Emma was probably asleep, darlin'," he explained.

"I really wanted to show her the birthday present you got me," she said proudly, her face beaming at the thought of her new, hand-tooled leather saddle. On each side the initials JB were branded into the design. Jessie had felt grown-up and special when her father surprised her with this one-of-a-kind gift. He'd already given her plenty of things she'd placed on her birthday wish list, including many of the books and videos she'd requested. But when they'd entered the stables this morning and she'd seen the new saddle already on her horse's back, she had jumped for joy.

"She'll be awake by now, won't she?" Jessie prodded.

Burke checked his watch. "I assume so."

"Then let's go back home so I can show her."

Burke turned his horse around and they headed for the house. He marveled at how quickly his daughter had taken to Emma. Jessie responded to her on a personal level, accepting her as an individual, not just as her uncle's lady friend.

His little girl, who wasn't so little anymore, liked and trusted this woman. He could tell from the way Jessie spoke about her. Jessie led with her heart, letting her head follow. Unlike her father, who'd learned the hard way to protect himself by letting his head guide his actions.

It didn't take them long to arrive back at the main house. When they did, Jessie begged, "Go get Emma for me, won't you, Daddy?"

Burke acquiesced to his daughter's wish, handing the reins of his mount to one of the stable hands so he could go inside the house and seek Emma.

As soon as he entered, Burke saw his mother coming down the stairs. "Is Emma up yet?" he demanded in a soft voice.

"Yes, she is," Santina answered, her eyes narrowing at the look on her youngest son's face. "I took her a breakfast tray a little while ago."

"Good," he said, mounting the stairs two at a time.

"Why the hurry?" Santina asked as he made his way past her.

Burke paused, one hand on the carved railing, and turned back to face his mother. "Jessie wants to show off her new saddle to her uncle Clay's girlfriend."

"Is that all?"

Burke gave his mother a puzzled glance. "What else could there be?"

"I don't know," she said, her eyes focused on him. "You tell me."

"There's nothing to tell, Mother."

Santina's instinct was rarely wrong when it concerned her children. Something was bothering Burke. She could sense it, see it in his face. He was well past the age when Mommy could make it all better, but that didn't stop her from wanting to alleviate whatever it was that was troubling him. Santina doubted that she'd ever get over that feeling, no matter how old her boys were.

A mother lion, her beloved Noah had once called her. She wryly acknowledged the truth of that. Now it would seem that one of her pride was hurting, and she suspected the problem was deeper than a mere thorn in the paw. She feared it was a thorn in the heart—long, sharp and capable of extreme damage.

"Clay called this morning."

Burke's posture stiffened slightly. His voice, when he spoke, was carefully neutral. "When's he arriving?"

Santina let out a sigh. "He's not."

"What?" Burke couldn't believe what his mother had just said. It was one thing to put the family second to business matters, but to ignore the woman he wanted to marry as well?

Damn Clay!

"What the hell is he thinking of?" Burke demanded in an angry tone. "Because it certainly isn't Emma's feelings. Did he even consider her at all?"

"He didn't do it deliberately, Burke," Santina stated, observing her son's ready defense of his brother's girlfriend. "It just couldn't be helped. You know what he thinks of her."

"Well," Burke responded scathingly, "what Clay thinks and what he does are two different things, Mama. Now, if you'll excuse me, I'll see if Emma wants to come outside and see Jessie's present." He turned and continued up the stairs.

"What's wrong?" Noah Buchanan came up behind his wife and slipped his arms about her slim waist, pulling her to his still hard body, nuzzling her neck.

"Burke," Santina murmured, enjoying the feel of Noah's lips on her skin.

"Burke?"

"Yes," she said, her tone anxious.

"Did he say something to you?"

"No."

"But you've got a hunch?"

She nodded her head.

"So tell me."

"I don't know how to explain it," she said. "But there's a difference in him. It's in his eyes, mostly. I see a new awareness."

Her husband paused in his actions. "Awareness of what?"

"That he isn't made of stone."

Noah lifted his head. "Stone?"

"Yes," she stated. "For far too long our youngest has clung to the belief that his emotions, save for a few exceptions, were best hidden beneath a layer of granite. Now I think Burke is discovering that this is no longer true."

"You're not saying what I think you're saying, are you?" Noah asked.

"That there's a woman involved in this transformation?" Santina nodded. "Yes."

Noah took a deep breath, letting it out slowly. "Clay's girlfriend." It was a calculated guess.

Santina nodded her head in agreement. "You know what's ironic, my love?" she asked, leaning her head back on Noah's shoulder. "I've prayed for so long that Burke would find a woman he could love. Remember what we were told as children? Be careful what you wish for—you may get it."

Burke was making his way down the hallway just as Emma closed the door to her room. He was continually captivated by her fresh beauty. Her skin glowed with health, her cheeks with a natural blush. It was all he could do to restrain himself from reaching across the small distance that separated them and helping himself to her soft mouth.

"Good morning."

His voice sent shock waves of pleasure rippling through her. Emma repeated his greeting, then added, "I was getting ready to take a walk."

Burke's gaze took in her outfit, the same one she'd worn when she first arrived at the ranch. "Great. Jessie wants to show you something. She's waiting for us outside."

Us. Burke's linking them together was bittersweet music to her ears. "What is it?"

A half smile touched his wide mouth, melting Emma's resolve to maintain a polite distance. "I'd better let her show you. There will be hell to pay from my daughter if I steal her thunder."

"Fine," Emma murmured, falling into step behind Burke as he turned and made his way back down the stairs. As she followed, she wished vainly that it was as an "us" that they went to meet Jessie. Hand in hand, hearts linked, a family.

It was crisp and clear outside, the sun warm, already melting the traces of snow on the ground. Renegade barked and bounded over to them, happily weaving his way between Burke and Emma, basking in the attention of both.

Emma matched her stride as best she could to Burke's longer one, anxious to see Jessie. As they came around the corner of the house, they met the girl leading her horse toward them, a big grin on her pretty face.

"Happy birthday, Jessie," Emma said, giving in to instinct as she hugged the child.

Jessie hesitated for a brief instant, then responded in kind, her arms tight around Emma's neck. Then she relaxed. "Look what Daddy gave me, Emma. It's a new saddle. All my own. See?" She pointed to the initials in the leather. "Isn't it neat?"

Emma nodded. "It certainly is." She ran her hand over the workmanship, feeling the various textures and indentations of the leather beneath her fingers. "So beautiful," she said.

Burke sucked in his breath as he watched Emma's fingertips slowly slide across the saddle. Her touch was light, gliding. He wanted desperately to feel her touch on his own skin. His body automatically hardened in response to his erotic thoughts as desire flared brilliantly to life.

"I've got something for your birthday as well," Emma stated, stepping back from Jessie's horse, a smaller version of Burke's own mount. "Not as grand as what your daddy got you, but I hope you'll like it nonetheless."

Jessie's face lit up. "Can I see it now?"

"If you'd like," Emma responded.

"Oh yes," Jessie said enthusiastically, her braids swinging as she bobbed her head, "I'd like that a lot."

Burke laughed at his daughter's reveling in her birthday gifts. Life could be so simple at Jessie's age. "Then take Pumpkin back to the stables," he instructed her, "and when you're done, we'll meet you inside." He checked his watch. "It's almost time to get changed for dinner, remember?"

"Okay, Daddy," Jessie said eagerly, leading her horse in the direction of the large stables. "I'll be right there, I promise."

After Jessie was out of earshot, Burke said, "You didn't have to get her anything."

"I know," Emma said, her eyes meeting his. She was tantalized by the unexpected warmth she saw there. "But I wanted to. Sometimes that's half the fun for someone her age, getting something totally unexpected."

Or, she added mentally, discovering something unexpected, like the way Burke's eyes crinkled at the corners when he smiled, or the small band of dusky freckles that dotted the bridge of his nose, barely visible unless one was standing close.

"Still, it was nice of you to think of her."

"No problem," Emma acknowledged. "It was my pleasure entirely." *Pleasure.* That was another word she was beginning to connect with Burke. The pleasure she garnered just by being in his company, by sharing time with him. Emma was storing these moments so that later, when she was alone, she could take them out and replay them as often as she liked. Hopefully, they would soften the innumerable lonely hours to come.

"Meet me in Jessie's room," Burke instructed as they walked back into the house. He gave Emma directions to his daughter's bedroom and strode off toward the kitchen.

Emma almost floated back up the stairs, she was so happy. Ridiculous to feel this way, she chided herself, but she couldn't help it. It felt so good to be in Burke's company, no matter what the reason, and she found that she couldn't deny herself any excuse to savor the moments she managed to grasp.

Inside her bedroom, she stripped off her jacket and hung it back in the closet. From the bottom of the closet, she removed a brightly wrapped package, replete with a large bow. She hoped that Jessie liked the gift she'd chosen. When Clay had told her about his niece's birthday, Emma had decided to get the girl what she hoped would be a special present, something different to remember her by. She'd been hard-pressed to come up with something unique that she thought Jessie might like. Since she had no experience in shopping for a girl almost a teenager, Emma went with an item that had caught her eye in a specialty store in Santa Fe.

Added to that gift was a simple pencil portrait she'd sketched of Jessie. Later, when she was back in her own studio, Emma would make her a more formal painting, but for now she was sure this would please Jessie. And, she hoped secretly, Burke as well.

Gathering the presents, Emma made her way along the hall to the other side of the house and Jessie's room. The door was ajar, so she didn't knock. Instead she called out, "Jessie?" and proceeded into the room.

Jessie was seated at a small desk facing one wall, talking on the phone. In one hand she held a box. "I love them, Uncle Drew," she said into the receiver. "They're so pretty. I'll wear them today, I promise." Jessie put the box back on her desk. "Yes, I miss you, too. When are you coming home?'' She sighed, a slight frown twisting her lips. ''That long?'' Then the little girl nodded her head at something the caller said, her face suddenly lighting up.

Emma placed the gifts on Jessie's bed, thinking now how well her choice would fit in with the decor of the child's room. The bed was a rustic canopy, with exposed posts that looked like they were made of bleached pine. Cowhide rugs were scattered about the floor; small brass horses decorated the windowsill, along with a vase of fresh flowers. Jessie's bed was done in shades of navy, cream and red, with assorted pillows portraying cowboy scenes. At the foot rested a sturdy Southwestern patterned blanket.

Above her desk, Emma noticed an unusual bulletin board. Various pieces of old, weathered boots were nailed into the wooden frame, forming a unique pattern. Several ribbons were tacked to the pegboard, along with cards and pictures of teenage TV stars. On the desk, several silver-framed pictures shared space with books and magazines. One of the photos, Emma noted, was identical to that in the album Santina had lent her—the picture of Burke holding Jessie. Another frame held a photo of her grandparents; still another, her father and uncles. Emma couldn't help but think that they were all handsome men, each in a different way.

''I'll tell Daddy you said hello. Goodbye,'' Jessie said, hanging up her phone. She turned around and saw Emma standing there. ''Want to see what my uncle Drew sent me?'' she asked. Not waiting for an answer, she produced the box and held it out to Emma for her inspection.

''They're lovely,'' Emma agreed. Inside the velvet box was a pair of delicate gold-and-topaz earrings, obviously old and obviously expensive. Emma recognized the Asprey name on the box. Jessie's uncle had a good eye for quality.

"And Uncle Clay gave this to me," Jessie said proudly, showing off the new watch she wore. It, too, was gold, smart and slim.

"Your uncles have great taste," Emma stated.

"You know what?" Jessie asked in a confiding tone, "I still like what my daddy got me the best."

Emma smiled at the girl. "You know what?" she answered. "So do I." She gestured to the presents on the bed. "I kinda hope that you like mine, as well."

Jessie got up from her chair and jumped onto her bed. Emma watched her start to rip open the wrapping paper.

At that moment, Burke entered, a small wooden tray in his hands. It held three tall, clear glasses with steam coming from the top. "Hot chocolate?"

He strode into the room and placed the tray on the desk, pushing aside some of the items to make room. He handed Emma one glass, and he took another. When he saw her look curiously at the paler liquid within, he said, "It's hot chocolate, all right. White chocolate."

Emma had heard of this new variation and was eager to try it. She sipped the beverage, enjoying the shavings of dark, bittersweet chocolate and the whipped cream that topped the drink.

Burke sipped his own and watched as a white, foamy mustache appeared on Emma's top lip. He had a sudden, intense urge to lick her mouth clean, his tongue removing the foam slowly. The drink would flavor the inside of her mouth as well, making it even sweeter, more tempting.

Their eyes met, and he could have sworn that Emma could read his thoughts. Why else did flags of color suddenly spring to her cheeks?

Kisses flavored by chocolate. Body decorating in whipped cream.

Good God, Emma wondered, *where are these ideas coming from?* Her imagination was taking a wild, overtly sensual turn. Burke was raising her body temperature and turning her inside out and upside down just by standing there, sipping hot chocolate.

Their eyes locked. Surely he couldn't read her mind? Heat swelled within her.

It was Jessie's voice that broke the spell. "Thank you, Emma. I love it!"

Emma blinked and turned her attention to the girl, who held the Hopi kachina doll carefully in her hands.

"Look at her, Daddy. Isn't she lovely?" Jessie showed Burke the doll.

Burke managed to tear his gaze away from Emma and focus on his daughter. "Beautiful," he whispered. Like the woman who'd purchased her.

Jessie scrambled from the bed and hugged Emma. "I love her."

Once again Emma tightened her arms about the girl, wishing for one crazy moment that Jessie was hers. It was as easy to love this child as it was her father. She closed her eyes for a second with that thought, then abruptly opened them.

Seizing upon time as an excuse, she said, "I've got to change." She reached past Burke and placed the glass back on the tray, then hastily made her way out of the room.

"Oh, Daddy, look. Emma did a picture of me as well." Jessie handed the sketch to her father.

Burke stared at the replication of his daughter, caught by Emma's skilled hands. His thumb softly brushed across the signature at the bottom as his mind grappled with the truth he'd been ignoring.

He'd fallen in love with Emma Cantrell.

the strength of the story of the family and the family's strength renders the book as important through an important subject and the brisk pace of some narrative as

Chapter Nine

It was a Thanksgiving unlike any Emma had ever experienced. This one was packed with family and laughter, with warmth and love. Used to a more solitary pursuit of the day, she found the gathering of Buchanans and assorted relatives a wonder both to behold and to be a part of.

She was welcomed into the fold by numerous aunts, uncles and cousins and treated as if she were already a member of the family, which aroused a number of feelings within her. Part of Emma felt guilty, as if she were there under false pretenses. Only she knew that she wouldn't be marrying Clay, that her inclusion into the Buchanan family circle was at best a ruse.

The other emotion she felt was joy. Having never been in such a situation, Emma was overwhelmed by the sheer power of this clan. It brought home to her how much she'd missed as a child, and even into her adult years.

There was a shared strength in belonging to a large group that cared about all the members of the familial unit. It was fascinating to observe how everyone, from the youngest toddler to the oldest adult, interacted.

Gradually, Emma was seized with a loneliness she'd never known before. She would miss this place when she left. She would miss the people, the closeness, the sense of being a part of a much greater whole.

At dinner, which was held in the larger, more formal dining room to accommodate all the family gathered, Emma was seated next to Burke and across from Vicky and Joe. Even in this large crowd she felt a sense of intimacy. When her napkin dropped to the floor, Burke reached it first. Their fingers met as he handed it back to her. Once more a sharp stab of awareness hit her when their flesh connected.

If only things were different. If only she could have squeezed Burke's hand in thanks, or reached out and stroked that tautly muscled thigh, a willing invitation for things to come.

But she couldn't.

Emma was so conscious of him sitting next to her—of each breath he took, every movement he made. She watched him help himself to a generous portion of the jalapeño cornbread stuffing, saying as he passed it along to her, "Be warned. This stuff can be as hot as a summer day in Texas."

Hot. Just like desire could be hot, Emma had discovered. Sharp. Pungent. With a kick all its own.

Next came a dish of orange-cranberry relish. "This is spicy," he murmured as he handed it to her.

Emma imagined Burke's kisses would be the same. Tangy, with a sweetly tart flavor. Utterly delicious. A sensation to be savored.

"White or dark?" he asked.

How could such a simple question make her toes curl in her boots? "White," she responded.

"Hand me your plate," he commanded softly.

Emma did as Burke requested. He gave it back to her with thick slices of succulent turkey breast, surrounded by roasted root vegetables. Substantial comfort food, as solid and nourishing as Emma imagined Burke's love would be.

Some lucky woman would find comfort and shelter in those strong arms, a partner to share the good and bad times with. A man for all seasons.

It just wouldn't be her. No matter how much she wanted it. No matter how deep her hunger.

She thanked him politely and set about eating her dinner.

Amor prohibido.

Forbidden love.

God, had it only been several hours ago that Burke realized how much he'd come to care for his brother's woman? In that short span of time his life had turned inside out. What had happened to his initial distrust of this stranger? His skepticism?

They had melted slowly during the hours he'd spent in Emma's company. Still, this feeling was so new that Burke wondered if he could trust it. Was it a resurgence of his youthful folly? Was he once again becoming blinded by the facade of a beautiful face and form? Or was he simply confusing old-fashioned lust with something stronger? Something deeper?

Burke didn't really think so. For one thing, he wasn't a boy any longer, capable of being fooled, of having his trust manipulated quite so easily. And what he felt for

Emma wasn't just desire, although that was a part of it. Though he'd been attracted to other women, this was distinct. His feelings were purer, cleaner, stronger, deeper. Emma wasn't merely a warm body he wanted for a few hours to pass the time, or to simply satisfy a need. He wanted her for the rest of his life.

Trouble was, so did Clay. And he had a prior claim. For Burke, that meant he would back off now while he could. While he was capable. Before he let something slip that might betray how he felt.

Pride strengthened his resolve. He wanted no one's pity or concern for the situation he found himself in. He would handle whatever came by himself.

Pride, albeit secret, was also a factor in Burke's assessment of Emma's artistic talent. Before sitting down to dinner, Jessie had shown everyone assembled her birthday portrait. His relatives had oohed and aahed over it, proclaiming their delight in the work. Jessie's spirit had been captured in that pencil sketch. Emma's eye was true and on target. He suspected it was because she saw his daughter as a real person instead of an underdeveloped adult. There had been an instant rapport between them that surprised him. He'd even wondered if Emma had been faking it so that she'd come off well in his family's eyes. He had tossed that notion aside the few times he'd seen the two of them together. Their liking was genuine.

"I can't wait to see what Jessie picked out for her birthday cake," Emma whispered to Burke as she accepted a cup of hot coffee.

"Knowing my daughter's sweet tooth, I'm sure it'll be something that could raise a person's blood-sugar level a thousand percent just by looking at it," he responded.

Emma laughed softly. Burke found himself thrilled by the sound. It was real. Delightfully so. So far he'd discovered nothing artificial about this woman.

And she was good with Jessie. Emma would, he thought, make a caring mother. Which was just as well, since Clay wanted children.

Burke glanced sideways at Emma while she was busy talking to one of his aunts. How would she look swollen with child? Glowing, he would imagine. Her skin, already beautiful, would be that much brighter. Her eyes would shimmer with the knowledge that she was helping create a miracle within the confines of her body. Somehow he didn't think she would be anything like Celia, who had constantly complained that she was miserable, that the baby she carried would ruin her figure permanently, that she hated her condition. If it had been up to Celia, she would have continued smoking and drinking heavily throughout her pregnancy, little caring what effect it had on the health of her child. He'd had to bribe her to quit both.

However, that was the past.

What he had to face was the present.

Suddenly, the lights in the room were dimmed and a silver cart was wheeled into the dining room by a smiling woman in her late thirties. Married to one of the ranch hands, she earned extra money by helping out at the main house when needed, like today. Three elaborate cakes rested on top of the cart, and assorted pies took up the second and third shelves. Candles proclaimed Jessie's age on each cake.

"Time to blow out the candles, darlin'," her father declared. "Be sure and make a wish."

Jessie, her long brown hair pulled back with barrettes so that her new earrings were visible, pushed back her chair and walked to the cart. She took a deep breath and looked at the large table filled with people, some of their faces in shadow. She spotted her father, and sitting beside him, Emma. Her mouth curved into a grin as she let out three puffs of air and blew out all the candles.

Burke left his seat to hug his child, followed by his mother. "What did you wish for?"

Jessie threw him an exasperated look. "You know I can't tell you, Daddy. It won't come true then."

"Sorry, darlin'." Burke thought it must have been an extra special wish if his daughter was determined to keep it to herself. Usually, Jessie confided in him.

"That's okay," she said patiently. "You just forgot that I'm not a little girl anymore."

Burke was surprised by the tone in his daughter's voice. He smiled as he laid his hand on her hair. "You'll always be my little girl, sweetheart, no matter how old you get," he whispered to her.

"Now," Santina said, picking up one of the silver cake knives as the lights were brightened, "who's for a slice of birthday cake?"

Acting on Vicky's suggestion that they take a break from the formal dinner, Burke and Emma, along with Vicky and Joe, carried their desserts down the hall and up the stairs to the large former nursery, which had been converted into a game room.

Stepping into it, Emma had the sense that she'd gone back in time to a gentlemen's club of a bygone era. It was paneled in dark wood, with two tables used exclusively for card games. English hunting prints hung on the walls. Dominating the middle of the room was a huge billiards table.

"Do you play?" Vicky asked Emma.

"Not really," she responded, peering a little closer at several of the prints, inspecting the detailed work of the painter.

Vicky shrugged her slim shoulders and took a seat in one of the comfortably padded wing chairs. The tartan print blended well with the room's decor. "I'm passable, that's all," she admitted. "Joe and Burke are what I'd call real hustler quality, though."

"Hustler quality?" Emma asked, raising her brows as she took the other wing chair.

"Oh yes," Vicky said, swiping a finger along the icing on her slice of cake. She'd put her china plate on the Regency side table between the chairs. "They're both good." Before Vicky could lick the icing off, Joe was there, lifting her hand to his mouth instead.

Emma watched the sensual byplay as Joe popped Vicky's index finger into his mouth and sucked the frosting from it in a natural and loverlike gesture.

Emma lifted her eyes. She met Burke's across the width of the billiards table as he was setting it up for a game. They held contact for mere seconds.

Hastily, Emma dropped her gaze, focusing on her own slice of cake. It was chocolate, covered with white frosting and a bouquet of confectionary bluebonnets and Indian paintbrushes for a uniquely Texas-style birthday cake. She lifted her fork and scooped off a bluebonnet. That, she figured, was much safer than staring at Burke, contemplating him and a dollop of frosting.

As he racked the balls on the table, Burke couldn't help but notice the way Emma's gaze skittered away from him. Instead, she focused on her dessert, her spoon delicately lifting the icing flower off, as if that were somehow important. He watched as she tasted it, her eyes closed in obvious enjoyment.

Get a grip, Buchanan, Burke mentally chastised himself. You're getting all worked up over how this lady eats a damned slice of cake. You're losing perspective.

"Ready, Joe?" he asked, his voice a husky growl.

"Yeah," Joe responded, stealing a kiss from Vicky before he joined Burke at the table.

When she thought sufficient time had passed so that Burke wouldn't notice, Emma allowed herself to stare at him between bites of cake. She admired the way he played the game, coolly and relentlessly. He methodically placed his shots, sizing up his opportunities, before driving home his advantage. His face was once again a study in intense concentration. Burke used his cue like a lethal weapon, his left arm mechanically responding. He'd pushed up the sleeves of the cream-colored sweater he was wearing. The thick gold-and-lapis bracelet on his left wrist gleamed in the low lighting. Emma yearned to feel the shape and texture of that particular piece of jewelry, then follow the path of his arm upward beneath the sweater. His skin would be warm, solid.

"Did my aunt Maria rope you into her pet project?" Vicky inquired as she cheered Joe on when it came time for him to shoot. "She can be as relentless as a Texas twister when she's of a mind to."

Her thoughts diverted, Emma gave a start. "I'm sorry, but what was it you asked?"

Vicky willingly repeated her query.

Emma answered, "She did make a strong pitch for my participation in her annual Christmas charity event."

Vicky snickered. "I thought as much."

"It's a good cause."

"The best," Vicky agreed without reservation. "Helping children. With so many budget cuts, things like arts programs are usually considered expendable. Some bureaucrats think it won't matter to a child. Thankfully Maria, along with others, thinks differently. Santina and I have already volunteered a free consultation and design to the highest bidders." Vicky glanced in her boyfriend's direction. "Joe's giving a cabinet. It's all done by auction. You bid on whatever you want."

"Yes," Emma said. "Your aunt explained that to me. She asked if I could be persuaded to donate a piece of artwork."

"Will you?"

"Yes," Emma said enthusiastically. "I believe in what she and her committee are trying to accomplish."

"Great. Are you planning to come to the auction?"

Emma ran her hand through the back of her hair, ruffling the curls. "I hadn't really thought about that."

"You should. San Antonio is lovely then. The streets are all decorated and lit up. It's so beautiful," Vicky said. "Besides, as I'm sure Clay's told you, the Buchanans have a house there, so there'd be no problem getting a room so close to Christmas."

Clay.

Emma lowered her eyes. The feeling of being an imposter was creeping over her again. How could she continue to let Vicky, and the rest of Clay's family, think that there was a future for them? She wanted to tell Vicky right now. She wanted desperately to let Burke know. Not that it would matter one way or the other to him, she was sure, but it would make her feel better. Less like a cheat.

However, it wouldn't be fair to Clay to tell his relatives that they were only good friends before she had a chance to explain the fact to him. She owed him that much. She owed him more: honesty. But it was the one thing she couldn't give Clay right now. Maybe some time, when she had the proper distance from her feelings for Burke.

Would that time ever come?

It had to.

"Well, if you decide to come, let me know," Vicky remarked. "We can have dinner or something."

"I'll have to check my schedule when I return home," Emma said, knowing that she wouldn't make promises she might not be able to keep. She liked Vicky and wanted to continue this burgeoning friendship, but she doubted that the other woman would feel the same way after Emma dumped Clay. Vicky would be loyal to her cousin. Emma understood that. Unfortunately, it didn't make her feel any better.

"Do that, then call me," Vicky insisted.

Emma placed a cheerful smile on her face, hiding the hurt. "Of course."

"Hey you two," Joe called out. "What say we have a little team playing?"

"Sounds like fun," Vicky agreed, getting out of the chair with Joe's helping hand. "Come on, Emma."

"As I said before," she repeated, "I'm not real good at this."

"Oh, who cares?" Vicky laughed as she took a cue from Joe's hands. "This is just for fun."

"Speak for yourself, Cousin," Burke chided. "I play to win."

"You gotta lose sometime, Burke," Vicky retorted.

Burke chalked his stick. I already have, Vicky, he thought. More than you'll ever know.

Emma reluctantly joined them, finding herself paired with Burke. She was uncomfortable and unable to relax. Whenever he came near her, she froze. Afraid of revealing too much, she overcompensated, remaining stiff and formal.

Burke picked up on it immediately. It was easy to read in the polite phrases she used, in her body language. When their hands touched as he showed her how to use the cue stick to best advantage for a shot, he felt Emma pulling back, as if his nearness offended her.

That hurt in a way he'd never been hurt before. It was sharp, like the slice of a blade on his skin. Deep enough to wound.

Consequently, he lost his focus on the game, allowing Joe and Vicky to trounce them.

Hell, it was just as well. He had to get out of there. Go somewhere where Emma wasn't. Simple as that.

"I reckon it's time we rejoin the family," he stated as he replaced the cue sticks in the wall cabinet.

"You're probably right," Joe conceded. He wrapped his arm around Vicky. "Let's go."

Emma watched as Joe and Vicky led the way back to the family. All she wanted to do was steal away and hide. Lick her emotional wounds in private. Be anywhere Burke wasn't. She'd never imagined that it could be so hard not to show feelings, not to give in to gut instincts. She was strung tight as a wire and feared she would snap from the pressure of ignoring what her heart told her to do: reach out to him, tell him, show him.

She had all but come unglued every time Burke's hand touched hers during the game. When his body was so close that she could feel the heat of his skin, smell the scent of his after-shave, it took all her willpower not to lean into him, relax and enjoy the masculine grace he possessed. It would have been all too easy.

Reality dictated otherwise. She would maintain the status quo just as she planned until it was time for her to leave. No one must ever suspect the true state of her feelings.

Emma realized that she would miss these people when she left. In a remarkably short time they'd become like real family to her. She loved their warmth, their generosity of spirit, their willingness to make a place for her in their lives.

But most of all, she would miss one special person— Burke.

The hours had slipped by slowly. The relatives had finally returned to their respective homes. Jessie was in bed; Santina and Noah were ensconced in the den, enjoying their own company; Emma had retired to her room almost an hour ago.

Burke had retreated to his office, away from everyone—most especially away from Emma Cantrell. He sat there, nursing his third bottle of beer. It was dark. A single Stickley lamp on his desk provided what little illumination there was in the room. A Vivaldi cello concerto floated through the air, the lush, sweet sounds a backdrop to his pensive mood.

Restless, Burke arose from his massive desk chair. He strode across the room until he was standing before the tall French doors that led outside. Within seconds, his dog had joined him, a silent, steady companion.

Burke felt constrained, as if invisible wires impeded his movements.

It didn't matter that he tried to make his mind a blank, wiping all traces of Emma from it like erasing chalk from a blackboard. Memories of her kept filtering back, each one stronger than the last.

She'd done her best to avoid him the rest of the evening. She was careful never to get too near unless it couldn't be helped. Emma was keeping her distance, both literally and figuratively. Why? What had he done to her?

He'd observed her throughout the night. Whenever he could, he'd tried to catch a glimpse of her without attracting any notice. He would look for the long swirl of her golden-brown suede, midcalf-length skirt, or spy from the corner of his eye a flutter of ivory-colored lace that was the old-fashioned blouse she wore. Or he might catch a brief glance of brown, high-heeled, lace-up-the-front leather boots—the kind of footwear that made you want to take your time unlacing them.

His mother suspected that there was something amiss. She had come up to him at one point, asking in a concerned voice, "Are you okay?"

"Of course," Burke had said, masking his true emotions from Santina's probing eyes.

"It's just that you look as though something is troubling you." She touched his sleeve in a gesture of comfort. "I'd like to help if I can."

"Mother," Burke replied, laying his hand over hers, "you're imagining things."

"I don't think so," she insisted.

"Well, I do."

Undaunted, Santina had changed her tactics. "She looks especially lovely tonight, doesn't she?" There was no mistaking whom she was referring to.

Burke paused before answering, trying to interject a cool note into his voice. "Emma would be hard-pressed to look anything less than lovely, I'm sure, Mother."

"Your father and I have grown quite fond of her. And—" Santina gestured with a nod of her head "—it would appear as though she has won over your grandparents as well."

Burke focused his attention on where Emma sat. She was talking to his maternal grandmother, who was showing Emma each piece of the turquoise-and-silver jewelry she wore in abundance. He watched as his grandmother removed the heavy ring from her right pinkie and gave it to Emma. It was a chunk of turquoise set in braided silver.

Burke could tell Emma was demurring, but the old lady insisted. He knew from experience that his mother's mother was formidable when she put her mind to something. She must have won out because he finally saw Emma slip the ring onto her finger, admiring it.

"I wouldn't be surprised if Mama didn't ask Emma over to Rancho Montenegro to see her vast collection of silver and turquoise," Santina noted. "She rarely accords outsiders that privilege."

Burke merely nodded his head.

"Oh, it looks as though Maria and Trey are leaving," Santina had murmured. "I'd better go and say goodbye. Excuse me." She had taken a step away when she turned and said, "I meant what I told you, Burke. If you need to talk . . ." She'd let the sentence trail off as she walked away.

Remembering her odd behavior now, Burke ran his hand over Renegade's neck, ruffling the dog's fur. His mother hadn't mentioned Clay at all during their conversation. An oversight on her part? Or had it been deliberate?

Emitting a deep sigh, Burke turned around and walked back to his desk. He stood in front of Emma's painting, mesmerized again by the power and beauty inherent in the picture. Somehow, standing there, Burke felt closer to her.

At least here in this room some part of her was undeniably his.

The clock softly chimed midnight.

Emma sat curled up in a chair in the sitting room, attempting to finish a book. It was no use. Every time she imagined the tall, dark, brooding hero, her mind supplied a familiar face for the fictional character.

She'd borrowed the book from the Buchanans' library. Santina had quite a collection of romance novels in several of the floor-to-ceiling bookcases. Her "keepers," she'd told Emma. "Feel free to borrow any of them if you'd like."

Emma had done that before she went upstairs, hoping she could keep her thoughts focused on something other than her own concerns, if only for a few hours. She had been secretly pleased to discover all of Kate Reeves's work there, her own illustrations gracing the covers.

Unfortunately, reading the novel she'd chosen only further stirred up her already roiled emotions. Every dramatic scene between the literary couple took on greater significance. Tears welled in her eyes with the poignancy of several of the passages. She empathized with their pain and longing.

When she reached the first love scene—a torrid kiss between the honorable man and the equally honorable woman, who believed that their love could never be— Emma couldn't read further. It was too painful, too intense. She could imagine only Burke. She could hear only Burke.

She closed the book with a snap.

All roads in her heart led back to Burke.

They always would.

Chapter Ten

Two days had passed. Emma was resolved that by to-morrow, Sunday, she would leave the ranch, whether or not Clay had returned.

Events, and her heart, dictated that she must. Since Thursday evening, she'd purposefully avoided being alone with Burke, or for that matter, spending more time than was absolutely necessary with him. She'd managed yesterday and today to eat breakfast alone, and lunch was shared with Jessie and Santina. Dinner on Friday night involved the whole family, so Emma had put on her newly created mask of composure, pretending that everything was fine, that she didn't long for Burke Buchanan with a need that was a strong, consistent fire in her belly.

But today would be the ultimate test. His grandmother had called last night and invited Emma to come and view her collection of jewelry. Fascinated by the use of silver and stones to create wearable art, Emma couldn't deny herself the joy to be found in looking at Mrs. Montenegro's array of pieces.

The only drawback to the situation was that Burke would be accompanying her. Jessie was on a sleep-over at a friend's house, and Santina and Noah had flown to Dallas earlier to attend a charity function and wouldn't be home until dinnertime. So that left Emma no other choice than to accept Burke's offer to drive her.

She told herself that it would be for only a few hours and she could stand it. She would have to. Her own pride demanded that she not let Burke know how she truly felt. It would be far too embarrassing to see either pity or contempt in his dark eyes should he discover her secret.

She had used the time early in the day to take another ride across some of the property. It felt wonderful to gallop the sweet-tempered mare full-out for a while until they both were cheerfully exhausted. After that the pace was slow and steady, so that Emma could imprint the landscape in her memory. Occasionally, she would halt the horse and pull out a small leather sketchbook from her jacket pocket, making a few pencil drawings of a spot that intrigued her. She had come across a cowboy moving a small herd of what Burke had told her were Santa Gertrudis from one part of the ranch to another. Emma watched as the horseman and his dog worked as one unit to muster the cattle. She waved, and the cowboy tipped his Stetson as they passed out of sight.

It was then that Emma got the idea for a new painting set in the heyday of the Texas cattle baron. This would be the one she would donate for the charity auction. Somehow it seemed so apropos. She scribbled her

concept across one of the pages in her sketchbook, her
fingers flying as she used her own form of shorthand to
code the idea, blocking the action in quick, broad
strokes with her pencil.

Emma checked her wristwatch. It was time to head
back to the house and get ready for the trip to Rancho
Montenegro.

Tucking her sketchbook and pencil in the inside
pocket of her jean jacket, Emma set her Appaloosa on
a fast course for the homestead.

Burke cursed himself for a blasted fool. After maintaining a safe distance between himself and Emma Cantrell for over a day, he had willingly placed his head back
into the noose.

How could he have made such a damnably stupid
mistake?

Easy. He hadn't been able to say no to his grandmother. Of course, he admitted with a rueful grimace,
taking a large swallow of his iced tea, he also hadn't been
able to resist the chance to spend time with Emma.

In his enforced reclusiveness, Burke discovered that he
missed her company. Missed seeing the sparkle in her
eyes. Missed the warmth of her laughter, the way she
moved and the smell of her perfume. Missed the movements of her hands as she talked, punctuating a word or
phrase with dramatic emphasis.

In short, Burke missed all of Emma Cantrell whenever she wasn't near him: body and soul, heart and
mind.

He swore softly in frustration.

How in the hell was he going to get over her? How did
one forget the person responsible for a resurrection of
sorts? Her coming had shown him another side of him-

self, a side he'd believed had been frozen numb. Like a shining beacon of light, she'd illuminated the darkness surrounding his heart.

Burke heard the snap of the pencil he'd been holding in his left hand as it broke in two. The wood was splintered, with raw, jagged edges on both sides.

He stared at what he'd done.

With sudden insight, Burke realized that he was a lot like the pencil—strong until a force even stronger was applied. Then, if he couldn't bend, he would snap, and all his raw emotions would be on display like the fractured fragments of the pencil.

He was courting heartache by loving Emma Cantrell, but he couldn't help himself.

Burke considered it an ironic twist of fate. His youthful, impassioned vows that he would never let himself fall in love, never risk his affections again, were coming back to haunt him with a vengeance. He'd been so damned cocksure that he would always be in control, would always have the upper hand when it came to the crazy emotion called love. For him love, or what had passed for it all those years ago, had proven false. Only for certain people did love work.

Or so he'd believed.

Emma had smashed the citadel of his carefully guarded heart with one innocent look, one tender smile. She'd challenged and defeated his notion that love was an illusion, or at best, a gift bestowed on precious few individuals. He'd thought himself immune from the need, from the powerful hunger to express that love.

Burke now knew all too well that he was as human and susceptible as the next man to love's embrace.

That thought gave him little comfort as he sat at his desk. For in acknowledging that love, he also acknowledged that it was never to be.

Once, he'd cherished his sense of privacy, of personal space. Once, he'd reveled in his lack of a relationship and all the emotional baggage that entailed.

Now he knew the difference between being alone and being lonely. Emma had shown him that.

It wasn't a lesson he liked learning.

The drive to the Montenegro estate was made in virtual silence. Aside from an occasional question from Emma regarding that side of Burke's family, couched in purely impersonal terms, conversation was minimal, as if speaking would require more than either one was willing to give.

Emma realized it was probably for the best. After all, if they indulged in lengthy discourse, if they exchanged more personal information, it would make it harder to leave, as she knew she must. It was better, she thought, to keep the playing field level, or someone might hear her heart break.

Or she might be tempted to say to hell with propriety and confess her secret.

The blast of the Jeep's horn as Burke signaled to an approaching car woke Emma from her private musings.

Both vehicles slowed down. The driver in the black luxury sedan pressed the electronic control to lower his windows, as did Burke.

"*Buenos días,* Tio Alejandro."

The older man smiled, revealing a set of well cared for white teeth beneath a pencil-slim, black mustache. He returned Burke's greeting with gusto, adding a few other words that brought a blush to Emma's face. He was being quite lavish in his praise of her to his nephew.

"Enjoy your lunch with my mother, Miss Cantrell," Alejandro Montenegro said, his blue eyes alive with humor. "Mama has been looking forward to this afternoon."

"As have I," Emma declared, relaxing a bit with that information.

Alejandro threw a glance in Burke's direction. "Mama is forever complaining that she doesn't see enough of her Buchanan grandsons, so this day is doubly special for her. Twice in one week." A wink of his eye and a deep laugh accompanied that statement as he waved goodbye and sped off down the drive.

Burke shifted gears and stepped on the gas again. The vehicle responded quickly, the well-tuned engine purring along the drive that led to the Spanish-style hacienda.

"Your mother mentioned to me yesterday in passing that one of her brothers had a position in the Texas legislature. Doing what?" Emma asked.

"Tio Alejandro is a Texas state senator," Burke responded. "He has been for almost twenty years." He drove through the cedar-and-stone gates that led to the house. "Politics is very much in the Montenegro blood. My grandfather was a state senator for ten years, then a U.S. congressman for twelve terms before he retired."

"I'm impressed," she said with genuine admiration. "Politics is such a major commitment, not only for the person running for office, but for the family as well. Maybe, more so for them," she added thoughtfully. "I would think it tough to live in a fishbowl, surrounded by sound bites and opposing sharks."

Burke glanced quickly at her face. Her tone sounded convincing, but he wanted to see for himself the truth in her eyes.

It was there, refreshingly direct in the brief look she permitted before facing the other direction.

"Yes, it can be grueling," he disclosed, "and it demands so much, rather like a jealous mistress. At least," he stated, a slight hint of amusement lurking in his deep voice, "that's how my grandfather once explained it to me."

He parked his car beneath a magnificent live oak. By the time he got out of the vehicle and walked around the hood, Emma was already there.

With a wave of his hand, he indicated that she should precede him. His boot heels clicked against the old bricks that paved the walkway to the front door, where his grandmother stood, waiting for them.

Emma let out a soft gasp of wonder as her eyes took in the splendor of the grand house. It was as if time had stood still. Architecturally the house was a vision from another era, another culture, a distinct homage to the Mexican influence on Texas.

"Welcome to Rancho Montenegro, Emma," the venerable woman said in greeting, holding out her hands.

Emma placed her own hands in the other woman's, feeling the paper-smooth skin. There was an underlying strength to them that belied the woman's age. Her grasp was firm and sure, as was her personal sense of style. Tailored slacks of wool and a silk blouse, both in cream, and a sleek, side-parted bob were indicators that she wasn't the typical elderly lady who followed trends or formulas.

Emma liked that. This woman was unique—like her grandson.

She kissed Emma on each cheek, then ushered her into the large house.

Emma felt welcomed, not only by her hostess, but by the atmosphere of the house itself. It was warm and inviting, its cool, whitewashed interior decorated in shades of the earth: warm browns, deep greens, strong blues, milky creams and rusty reds. Large, terra-cotta tiles lined the hallway and led to a succession of rooms.

Maryanne Rayburne Montenegro was almost as tall as her grandson. She embraced Burke warmly, her arms enfolding him tightly. Then she placed a solitary kiss on his cheek, her hand caressing his face briefly. "It is always too long between your visits, my boy," she admonished him with a smile. "But it's well worth the reward for these old eyes to see you as often as I can."

She turned her attention to Emma. "And you," she said, her blue eyes sharp and inquisitive, "are just what my grandson needs. I'd almost given up hope he would find the right woman."

"Why, thank you," Emma responded politely. A shiver of guilt ran through her at the thought of the deception she was perpetrating on a nice person whose only concern was the happiness of her family.

Maryanne Montenegro dismissed what she considered false modesty with a wave of her beringed hand. "Just being honest, my dear. You'll find that I don't mince words." She picked up a large wicker basket loaded with blooms that lay on the hall table. "Do you garden?" she asked.

"Sorry." Emma shrugged her shoulders. "I don't have time. Besides," she added with a smile, "I think both of my thumbs are most certainly not green."

The other woman chuckled at Emma's remark. "Ah, time. The bane of us all." She shook her head. "That's too bad. It's one of my keenest pleasures. Remind me to show you my greenhouse before you leave today.''

Emma looked at the assorted roses in the basket. ''They're quite lovely,'' she murmured in appreciation.

''I thought they would look lovely on the table with our lunch.'' Burke's grandmother lifted the basket so that Emma could smell the delicate fragrances coming from several of the roses. ''They're my favorite flower,'' she said. ''Hardy. Beautiful. Adaptable. The essence of romance, if you ask me.'' She leaned over to whisper to Emma, a glint of mischief in her eyes, ''Always keep them in your bedroom, my dear. It does wonders for the mood.''

While Emma laughed at that remark, Burke's mind painted its own scene: an early morning spent lazily in bed, with Emma snuggled beneath his thick down comforter, half-asleep. From a nearby vase, he would remove one of the long-stemmed red roses, trailing it seductively down her exposed arm, across her bare shoulder, along her cheek. A shower of rose petals would cover the bed as she awoke fully, to the heady smell of perfume from the crushed blossoms. Smiling invitingly, her lips curved as if she held a secret, she would throw back the comforter, welcoming him with open arms, nothing between them but the sheets and the multicolored petals....

Burke inhaled sharply, the scent of the real flowers blending with those of his fantasy. He stared straight ahead and met the eyes of his grandmother. She nodded to him slightly with a knowing smile on her mouth.

What the hell was that all about? he wondered, puzzled by his grandmother's speculative regard.

''Come, help me arrange these, will you, Emma?'' Maryanne Montenegro inquired. ''Then I will show you my collection." She turned to Burke. "I'd like you to select a bottle of wine from the cellar for our meal."

Burke nodded. "What would you like Gran?"

"Something very special, I think. I leave it to your discretion."

He strode off in the direction of the wine cellar while Emma accompanied his grandmother into one of the smaller rooms off the hall.

Sunlight streamed through the windows as they entered, rays of light dancing along the well-polished mahogany table. Three places were set. In the middle of the table was a tall crystal vase the hue of warm gold. It was empty, waiting for the flowers to transform it into a radiant centerpiece.

A few snips from Maryanne's garden scissors and the roses were ready to arrange. The older woman picked out a few other flowers from the bottom of the basket to add contrast and color. Emma smiled as she watched the floral canvas take shape.

"Just like life," Maryanne said as she completed her task, standing back to survey the arrangement. "A little bit of this and that. It's all in the blending." She set her basket and shears on a nearby dresser, adding, "Surprising what works well together sometimes, isn't it?"

Without waiting for an answer, she continued, her gaze direct. "Like people. Sometimes the oddest mixtures work, don't you find? All it takes are the right ingredients, time and love. Nature and God do the rest."

"I suppose you could say that," Emma agreed, detecting a certain undercurrent to Burke's grandmother's remarks. It baffled her slightly, as if the older woman was deliberately couching her words. But why would she?

"Now come with me." Maryanne invited in her softest tone.

Burke found the two of them upstairs in his grandmother's sitting room. He recalled that as a child he had loved to play here when he came for visits, imagining himself an important figure in Texas history as he rode his antique wooden pony. Or some days he was a simple cowboy who got to ride to the rescue of the ladies, usually his mother and grandmother at tea.

He watched from the doorway as each piece of his grandmother's jewelry was lovingly unwrapped from the folds of material that protected it. The majority of her collection was on loan to museums and colleges throughout the state.

"These are the ones I couldn't bear to part with," he heard her explain to Emma as she handed the younger woman a necklace. Burke recognized the large squash-blossom pendant; the workmanship was a tribute to the artist's beliefs. Next came several rings of various sizes and textures, a mixture of corals and shades of turquoise all set in silver.

"Do try some on," Maryanne urged.

"I'd love to." Emma slipped on several of the heavy rings, admiring the craftsmanship of the Native silversmiths.

"What do you think of these?"

As Burke's grandmother pulled out several bracelets, Emma's eyes widened. She removed the rings and placed them back in their wrappings and cedar boxes, anxious to try the chunky wristbands.

Burke silently observed Emma trying, examining, appreciating the various pieces like an excited child discovering a treasure trove.

Gold. He would dress her in gold. As good as Emma looked wearing the silver, he saw her instead in warm gold. A bracelet to match his own, then a necklace and earrings, distinctly crafted for her alone. Something that said this woman was the most fascinating mixture he'd ever known—a soul that looked to the past; a heart that looked to the future.

Burke could see it all so clearly.

And just as clearly, overlapping his vision, Burke could see Clay slipping a wedding ring on Emma's finger.

That scenario was reality.

Hankering after a dream wasn't going to make it come true. Wanting it wasn't going to make it happen.

"Don't just stand there, Burke," his grandmother said when she looked up and found him lingering at the door. "Come on in."

Emma raised her head, her eyes meeting Burke's for the briefest instant before she lowered her lashes and pretended he was just another man, no one special.

Maybe if she told herself that often enough and long enough she might come to believe it someday. But not today. Today was reserved for wanting and longing, for needing and yearning for what couldn't be. It was a grab-all-the-sweet-memories-that-she-could day. There would be time enough for loneliness and regrets later. Plenty of minutes and hours to think about what might have been, what could have been.

The rest of her life.

"Thanks for giving me the opportunity to see your collection," Emma murmured softly as she handed back the last of the silver bracelets to Maryanne. "You've got good reason to be proud of it."

"I'm so glad you liked them." Maryanne repacked her trunk and locked it with a fancy key, itself a work of art in silver and turquoise. "I had a feeling that you would." She shot a glance at her grandson. "They're for Burke's girl, Jessie."

Emma was happy about that. She thought the little girl would love them, and more importantly, cherish them as much as her great-grandmother had. "A good choice," she agreed.

"Jessie's a lot like her daddy," Maryanne said lovingly. "A Texan through and through. She's proud of who and what she is. It's fitting that she have the silver." The woman fixed her gaze on Emma. "You did right well by her with that picture you gave her."

Emma smiled. "That was easy to do. Jessie's such a natural when it comes to posing."

"I'd like you to do another one for me. Nothing fancy, just the same as what you did for her. And you can name your own fee."

Emma demurred. "No," she stated unequivocally. "I don't want your money." She paused, taking a deep breath, then wet her lips. "Your family has shown me enormous kindness these past few days. Consider it my way of paying some of that hospitality back."

"Are you sure?"

"Yes. And maybe someday you'll sit for me," Emma proposed. "You'd make an interesting subject."

Maryanne was flattered, although hesitant. "I'm not so sure about that."

"Why not, Gran?" Burke asked. "Emma's a damned fine artist. I'm sure there are lots of people who'd jump at the chance to have her..." he paused, aware of the other meaning to his words "...paint them."

Emma responded warmly to his unexpected praise. "Thank you for the endorsement, Burke."

He shrugged his shoulders. "No problem. It's the truth." A smile accompanied his words. Small, but it was there.

At least he respected her as an artist, Emma thought, warming under the impact of that slight smile. That was something for as long as it lasted. She wondered what the reaction of his family would be when she broke things off with Clay. Whatever goodwill she'd managed to achieve might be shattered by the actions she would take, although she hoped not. Maintaining some sense of balance might be hard for Clay's family when they heard the news. To be fair, Emma couldn't blame them if they chose not to respond as well as she hoped.

"Our lunch should be ready by now," Maryanne declared, standing up. She observed the unmistakable hint of sexual tension in the air. On Thanksgiving day she had noticed subtle changes in her grandson. Today only reinforced that impression in her mind. This woman had a definite impact on Burke's life. Maryanne could read it in his face, hear it in the tone of his voice. The bitterness and disillusionment that he had lived with for so long seemed to be dissipating before her very eyes. And all in a matter of days.

Because of a woman.

This woman.

Luncheon with Maryanne Rayburne Montenegro was something else, Emma concluded. Burke's grandmother was delightful, filled with stories about her family and about Texas. Emma could have listened to her longer, especially whenever the older woman talked about Burke. Every little bit of information on him was carefully tucked away in Emma's memory so that it could be mnemonically examined whenever she wanted.

As the afternoon wore on, Emma felt more and more like bolting because of the ruse she was playing. She disliked pretending to this woman, to this family and to herself most of all that everything was as it should be. She was truly sick and tired of faking soon-to-be-engaged emotions.

What she wanted was someplace to lick her wounds in private. A chance to ostensibly get her head together and figure out her future plans.

Hard to believe that only days had passed and her world had changed so much.

"Would you like to go for a ride?"

Emma turned her head and looked at Burke as they made their way back home to the Buchanan ranch. More than anything she longed to say yes.

"No, thank you," she declined politely. "I've got a splitting headache." When in doubt, that excuse proved convenient and universal.

"That's too bad," he said. Burke got the message loud and clear. The lady didn't want anything to do with him. A headache was the oldest excuse in the book to avoid spending time with someone.

Fine with him.

Who was he kidding? Certainly not himself.

Emma sneaked a quick glance in Burke's direction. His features were taut, the knuckles on one hand showing white as he gripped the steering wheel. If she didn't know better she would suspect that he was hurt by her refusal to go riding with him.

Get real! her inner voice mocked. He's probably grateful that he doesn't have to play the gracious host any longer.

Yet if that were true, she countered, playing devil's advocate with herself, why was there so much tension in his body, in the confines of this car? If she could look into his eyes right now, what would she see? And what about his heart? If she could see into that...

But she couldn't. There was a clear sign posted there—No Trespassers Allowed!

Emma understood that message. She might not like it, but she respected it. And him. In so short a span of time she'd discovered love, desire, respect, admiration, affection—all wrapped in one man.

Too bad for her he was beyond her reach.

Chapter Eleven

Burke awoke with a start.

He reached out one hand and switched on the brass lamp that stood atop the bedside table. The soft, mellow light illuminated the darkness. He picked up his wristwatch and noted the time: almost dawn.

His sleep had been fitful. The white, goose-down comforter lay in a tangled heap, half on, half off the bed. All that concealed his nude body was a burgundy sheet, barely covering his lap and right leg. Burke lifted his right arm and tucked it behind his head, a soft sigh escaping his lips.

He'd lain awake for most of the night, his thoughts permeated by Emma Cantrell. When she'd refused his offer of another outing on horseback, Burke had accepted as gracefully as he could, hiding the disappointment he felt under a falsely calm exterior.

He should be grateful she didn't want to go riding with him. At least that's what he told himself. After all, did he really need the strain of pretending he was an impartial spectator when what he really wanted was to share so many things with her? When he wanted to hold her close and feel a responding leap of her pulse when he touched her, when he kissed her?

Instead, Burke did what he did best—buried himself in work. Checking and rechecking figures, going over inventory, entering stud records for both cattle and horses from a handwritten logbook to his new laptop computer. Doing whatever he could to keep his mind off Emma.

That hadn't proved possible.

He wanted to hold on to her, in much the same way that daylight this time of the year tenaciously clung to the land before surrendering to night. Their moments together played and replayed in his mind.

Emma was for him, Burke realized, a bringer of light, the redeemer of his misplaced faith in love. With all the skill of a surgeon, she'd cut through the cankerous bitterness and pain he'd clung to since his unfortunate union with Celia. His senses, purposefully dulled by years of rigid self-control, now flared to life with an intensity that was hard to ignore.

Yet ignore them he must, along with all the tender emotions he felt for her.

What a dilemma he found himself in—with no way out and no one with whom to share his thoughts. His best friend, the guy who'd always been there for him— his older brother Clay—was the last person in whom he could confide.

Noah and Santina were out of the question, too, because he couldn't put his father and mother in the untenable position of being forced to choose between their two sons.

Burke needed an objective, impartial ear—someone who wouldn't pass judgment, someone who would help him see all sides of this problem and figure out a solution. He needed blunt advice from a no-nonsense kind of person.

His lips curved in a smile. He knew just who he had to call. Why in hell hadn't he thought of him before?

He switched off the light, threw back the sheet and rose in one fluid motion. When he stood up, he gave his bed a penetrating glance, as if seeing it for the first time. Several moments ticked by. All this time he'd never understood just how lonely a king-sized bed for one could be.

He did now.

Emma awoke early as well.

Her suitcase was packed; her mind made up. Arrangements were already in place for her trip home. All the details were taken care of, so there was little to do until later that morning.

After rising, she slipped on her robe and made her way down the back stairs, which led directly to the kitchen. Emma suspected that there would be a pot of coffee brewing and she was right. Her only fear was of running into Burke at that time of the morning. She knew he was an early riser.

The thought of seeing him almost made her skip the coffee, but she needed it to give her a caffeine jolt, since she'd had so little sleep. Every time she closed her eyes, all she could see was Burke. Again and again he haunted her dreams, slipping in and out of them so easily.

She sipped from her large mug of steaming coffee and walked into the adjoining room in the bedroom suite. Curling up in the chair there, she thought about the conversation she'd had with Santina Buchanan last night.

After dinner, while lingering over coffee and dessert, Emma had approached Santina with her request.

"You're leaving so soon?" Noah had asked as he poured a small amount of cream into his cup.

Emma had raised her head, her eyes meeting Burke's across the table. His face was impassive, his eyes unreadable. The only indication that her statement had any effect on him was the slight flaring of his nostrils. Was he glad to see her go? Emma wished she knew.

She tore her gaze away from Burke's face—the one face she would never forget—to answer his father. "Yes. I have some work that needs to get finished, and, as much as I've enjoyed my stay here, it really is time for me to leave. I hope you understand."

"Why, of course we do," Santina responded, reaching out her hand and gently squeezing Emma's. "We've loved having you, and I know I speak for my entire family when I say that I hope you'll return soon. Maybe for Christmas?"

Emma shook her head. "I'm afraid that will be impossible."

"Oh, that's too bad," Santina murmured.

You won't think so later, Emma wagered.

"Could someone drive me into Derran, where I can rent a car?"

"You don't have to do that," Noah stated. "It's a simple matter for our pilot to take you anywhere you want to go."

"There's really no need," Emma protested. "Besides, isn't he with Clay?"

Noah shrugged his broad shoulders. "No problem. I'll give Clay a call and tell him to send Jim back."

"No, really, that's okay," Emma reiterated. "I don't mind driving."

Santina gave Emma an anxious look. "Are you sure about that? It wouldn't be any bother to see that you're taken anywhere you want to go."

Emma pushed away her plate, which held a half-eaten slice of pumpkin pie. "Yes, I'm sure. Thanks for the offer, but I'd rather drive."

"Then you just let me know when you want to leave and I'll drive you into Derran myself," Noah offered.

"Before ten, if that wouldn't be too much bother."

"No, that's fine by me."

Emma had been so afraid that Santina or Noah would suggest that Burke make the effort to see her safely to her destination, or that he would offer from a sense of loyalty to Clay. She sighed in relief when they didn't.

So now here she was, drinking coffee and still thinking about Burke. In less than three hours she would be leaving the ranch, putting this holiday behind her as best she could.

Emma wanted to talk to someone about the turn her life had taken these past few days. A sympathetic listener who could help her put things in perspective.

She also needed to be in her own home, safe from the whirlwind. A place where she could seek shelter from the upheaval. Somewhere that didn't have Burke's imprint, his quietly powerful life force constantly surrounding her. Someplace where she wouldn't hear the echoes of his deep voice or smell the scent of his woodsy cologne.

Emma wondered if such a place existed for her anymore.

God, she would have laughed out loud if a week ago
anyone would have told her that within a few days her
life would be thrown off balance so easily. Things like
that happened only in the movies, or in the romance
novels her friend Kate wrote. They didn't happen to
practical, focused people like herself, people who knew
where they were going in life.

She discovered her coffee was cooling off when she
took her next sip. She put her slippered feet to the floor,
cradling the mug in her hands. It was time for a hot
shower and breakfast, then her goodbyes.

That would be tough, Emma acknowledged—saying
farewell. Instinctively, she knew which would be the
hardest, the goodbye that would take the most out of
her.

Tears welled in her eyes and she blinked them back.

How did you say goodbye to love when you'd never
even said hello?

Three hours later, Emma's suitcase was safely ensconced in the trunk of Noah's pewter gray Cadillac.

Overnight the weather had taken a turn for warmth
and the temperature hovered around 73°. All the snow
had melted and there was a smell of freshness in the air.
Several mares and their foals gamboled in the nearby
paddocks. Emma reached into the pocket of her short
denim skirt and pulled out a napkin containing some bits
of dried apple that she had begged from the Buchanans' cook. She dumped the pieces into her hand and held
them out, calling softly to the animals. One mare and
her coal black colt ambled over and proceeded to feed
from her hand. She rubbed the mare's nose, then bent

down and stuck her hand through the wooden fence so the foal could have a share, too.

It was all so beautiful. So perfect. A place she was already growing to love.

"Gran told me that you were leaving today."

Emma stood up and turned around. Jessie was there, her head cocked to one side, hands stuffed into the pockets of her jeans.

"That's true, I am," Emma responded.

"Why? Don't you like it here?"

Out of the mouths of babes, Emma thought. "Of course I like it here, honey."

"Then why don't you stay?"

"Because I don't live here, Jess," Emma explained. "My home's outside of Taos."

"I'll bet that no one would mind if you moved in here," Jessie said hopefully.

Emma was touched by the child's sweet offer. Jessie couldn't know just how much Emma wished that she could stay. But if the child knew her father was the major reason she wanted to stay, would she still be so enthusiastic?

"That's awfully nice of you, Jessie, but I have a life elsewhere." Emma smiled and spontaneously held out her arms in invitation. The child responded and hugged her.

"I think I'm gonna miss you, Emma."

"Well," Emma said, her voice quavering slightly, "I know I'm gonna miss you, honey."

"Are you coming back real soon then to visit? You don't have to wait for Uncle Clay to bring you, do you?"

"I've got a pretty heavy schedule right now, what with gallery shows and commissions," Emma explained, resting one hand on Jessie's shoulder. "I doubt that I'll be back here for a while." If ever, she added silently.

"Can I call you?"

Emma wanted to refuse. It would be better to cut all ties while she could. She shouldn't encourage an association that Jessie's father would probably refute within the month. But Emma couldn't sever the connection. She was fond of Burke's daughter, and not just because Jessie was Burke's blood, though that was a part of it. Jessie was the kind of child Emma would like for her own daughter—bright, easygoing, fun and open. In spite of her parents' messy divorce, Jessie was able to laugh and give of herself. She responded to people honestly, as Emma longed to do but couldn't because of repercussions that would ensue.

"Of course you can. I'll give you my private number, and if you feel like calling me, then do so." Emma released the girl and searched in her small purse for a piece of paper and a pen. Then she wrote the information down, including her address. "Just in case you want to write me, too," she said as she handed Jessie the scrap of paper.

Jessie tucked it into the pocket of her jeans. "I'd like that," she said.

"Good. Then I'll look forward to hearing from you whenever you want."

Jessie scuffed the toe of her boot into the earth. "Can I ride with you into Derran?"

Emma grinned. "Of course."

"Is Daddy coming, too?"

"No, honey, he isn't."

Jessie shrugged her small shoulders. "Okay." She moved toward the fence, attempting to pet the foal, which then galloped off. "Are you going soon?"

"Yes." Emma looked toward the main house, in the direction of Burke's office. "I just have to say one last goodbye and then I'll be ready to go."

Burke stared at the blinking cursor of the laptop, in exactly the same spot as it had been for the last fifteen minutes.

It was useless. He wasn't getting a damned thing accomplished by sitting here like some lovestruck, idiot schoolboy. Every time he tried to focus on business matters, he saw Emma's face or heard her laugh.

What was really bothering him was that she hadn't said goodbye.

And why should she? he asked himself. He was nothing to her, except maybe a future brother-in-law.

Burke's left hand clenched into a tight fist, the knuckles showing white beneath the golden-toned skin.

Damn it! He wanted Emma to come to him, to not be able to leave the ranch until she saw him. He wanted her to recognize him as a man, as an individual, not just as her boyfriend's younger brother. While admitting the colossal ego that demanded, Burke didn't care.

He could go to her. He could seek her out and offer his good wishes for her future happiness with Clay. He could do that.

But he wouldn't. The lie would stick in his throat, choking him if he were to utter it. In exasperation, he tunneled his fingers through his hair.

Emma opened the door without knocking, knowing that she was being rude in doing so, yet not caring. She was afraid that if she knocked, Burke might refuse her entrance. Or simply ignore her.

Or worse yet, he might not even be there.

She found him sitting behind a massive desk, his head bowed, one hand burrowing through the short, sable locks.

Emma longed to run her own fingers through his hair.

Renegade, lying on the rug in front of the couch, lifted his head and looked at her. The dog eased himself off the floor and woofed in friendly greeting. He came over to Emma, and she bent down and ran her hand over his neck, ruffling his thick coat. Renegade sat there, his tongue lolling, accepting the tribute.

Hearing them, Burke jerked his head up, staring at the visitor. Emma rose slowly from her crouched position. Taking a deep breath, she quietly crossed the threshold, the dog at her heels.

"Hello, Burke." She walked slowly across the room until she stood in front of his desk. She quickly scanned the room, deemed it pleasing, finding it very much Burke. She liked the leaded glass doors of the bookcase that lined one wall. Just the right touch, as were the rest of the furnishings.

Above the bookshelves hung the portrait Santina had mentioned earlier. Emma's glance focused on the handsome and compelling couple as she stepped forward to examine the framed canvas. Recognizing the artist's name, Emma smiled and stepped back.

Turning her head, her eyes finally came to rest on the painting that hung on the wall behind Burke. *Hers.*

The breath caught painfully in Emma's throat. It looked so right there. The painting *belonged,* even if she never would. It had found its true home.

Emma recognized the stunning physical resemblance between the man in the room and the cowboy in the painting. The details were eerily similar to the reality she now knew. Like Pygmalion, she had fashioned her own male version of Galatea and fallen in love with the ideal come to life before her.

This painting had set her on a course of change in her life. It had given her a new creative vision and introduced her to a wealth of experiences. Through it, she had found love.

"Makes you believe in fate, doesn't it?" Burke asked, pushing back his desk chair, rising, his dark eyes drinking in the sweet sight of Emma here, in his domain. She wore the same sweater she'd had on the other night, the color flattering to her skin and hair. It was tucked into a short jean skirt that gave him the opportunity to admire the length of her legs. Her panty hose was sheer; Burke could see the dimple in one knee, the scars of an obvious accident on the other.

Blood pumped into his system faster and hotter. It pooled and tightened in his groin, pushing against the denim fabric. Aching sensations of longing tore through him.

Emma's voice, when she finally spoke, was husky. "Yes, it does," she said, answering his question. "Strange how these things occur." My God, she thought, she was babbling drivel just so she wouldn't confess what was foremost in her heart. Warmth that had nothing to do with the unexpected temperature outside heated her skin, centering in the lower portion of her belly. Her arms, hanging stiffly at her sides, ached to hold Burke; her mouth yearned to experience the raw stamp of his.

"Serendipitous."

"Exactly," she murmured, wondering what it would be like to rip open all the snaps of his dark blue, denim shirt. "As if you were meant to own it." The first two snaps were already undone, exposing the column of his strong throat.

"I've had that same thought many times." Recently, too many to count, Burke thought. Pleasure and pain. That's what the painting had brought him. The pleasure of admiring the beauty and power Emma had brought to life on the canvas. The pain of discovering love, only to deny its existence.

Emma realized that if she stayed here any longer she was going to cry. She could feel the tears now, welling inside her, threatening to spill forth—not quite a torrent, but an embarrassing flow all the same. As she stood there, her heart was breaking into smaller and smaller pieces, each one imprinted as if by a branding iron with his name.

"I just came to say goodbye." It took all her control to manage that one sentence.

"That's right, you're leaving today. I'd almost forgotten." He deliberately spoke the lines with a coolness he was far from feeling.

Emma swallowed the hurt that rose within her at his tone. Obviously, it was a matter of little importance to Burke whether she left the ranch or not. "I can quite understand," she acknowledged politely. "I know you're a busy man, even on a Sunday. But God Himself rested one day a week."

He ignored her comment, unsure of how to take it. "The ranch occupies a lot of my time, Sundays included, I'm afraid."

"And you wouldn't have it any other way, would you?"

Burke shrugged. "No, I wouldn't. It's my life, like I assume painting is yours."

If he'd asked her that only a few days ago, Emma would have said unequivocally yes. She couldn't state it for a fact any longer. Not after finding the one thing that could have taken its fair share of the abiding passion she'd reserved for her work. This timely visit had forced her to undergo a sea change, whether she wanted it or not. Life hadn't given her a choice. It presented her with a jolt that opened her eyes, awakened her heart and claimed her soul.

"It always has been," she admitted.

"Then you understand perfectly where Clay's coming from when he up and leaves you like he did," Burke stated.

"Yes."

"My brother is real lucky he found you." Burke's eyes met Emma's and held them for precious moments. He drank his fill, memorizing each detail.

Emma held his gaze, her own eyes marking the beauty to be found in his face. She would never tire of him as a subject for her work. Burke's visage would suit all mediums: charcoal, oils, pencils, pastels—it wouldn't matter. Whatever she used would be right for him. "I'm glad you think so."

"I do."

Emma supposed that she should say she was lucky, too, but she couldn't put another lie between them. Instead, she held out her hand.

Burke gripped the smaller, softer hand in his, holding it moments longer than he should, unable to let go right away.

Emma's skin tingled in reaction. Any minute now she was afraid that her knees were going to buckle. Wouldn't that be stupid? her inner voice mocked. Swooning like a heroine in a Victorian novel at the mere touch of a man's hand.

Stupid or not, it was how she felt.

Damn him!

Burke's next gesture took Emma completely off guard.

He leaned over, dipped his head and ever so gently kissed her cheek. "Goodbye," he whispered in that sexy voice. His breath caressed her skin.

Emma closed her eyes and savored the brief moment. That's all it was—a sweet, precious, stolen moment she would treasure. Opening them again, she faced the cold reality of the situation. It was time to leave. Now. Before she did or said something she would regret.

She smiled as best she could. "Goodbye, Burke." Turning, she made her way out of the office and out of his life.

He watched her go, his hands clenched into fists at his sides. It took all his considerable energy to hold back the words he wanted to utter. *Wait. Please stay. You can't possibly go until you hear what I have to say.*

Instead, he remained silent, letting Emma walk out the door, unaware of how he felt, unaware of what he wanted.

A sadness greater than anything he'd experienced before crept over him. Wanting to blot it out, Burke forced himself to move. He poured a large quantity of good Kentucky bourbon into a glass tumbler, tossing back a healthy swallow. Praying that it would numb the feelings that threatened to overwhelm him, he carried the almost-full bottle and glass back to his desk, Renegade at his heels. Burke sank into the leather chair, blindly staring straight ahead as the dog settled at his feet.

When he was done with that glass, Burke mechanically poured himself another.

It was going to be a very long day.

It was afternoon the next day when Emma finally awoke. She'd been so tired when she arrived home late the night before that she'd gone directly to bed, worn out from the drive and the emotional turmoil of the past few days.

She padded to her kitchen to fix herself something to eat. Scrambled eggs and toast was about all she cared for, so she made them, drinking two mugs of coffee while she prepared the food.

She was just sitting down at her kitchen table with her plate when the phone rang. There was a slew of messages on her machine, but she hadn't had the energy to listen, so she'd ignored them. Time enough for them later, she figured.

"Hello, sweetheart."

A Texas accent. A deep voice.

Her head snapped up. She paused with the fork halfway to her mouth.

"Are you there? If so, please pick up." It was Clay's voice. "God, but I miss you, Emma." There was a short pause. "Guess you're either asleep or in your studio. You'd just left when I called the ranch yesterday. Here's my number." He rattled off an area code and seven digits. "Call me."

The machine clicked off when he hung up.

Emma stared at the wall phone. She let out the breath she'd been holding, sighing deeply. For one crazy minute she'd thought it was Burke calling.

Fat chance.

She was on her fourth mug of coffee when she ambled back into her bedroom and curled up in the comfortable bed. Snuggling under the quilt, she sipped at the strong brew, wondering what *he* was doing right now.

Going on with his life, she assumed. Just as she had to do.

Easier said than done.

Chapter Twelve

"Are you sure that you're not just looking to have a hot itch scratched, little brother?"

Burke reacted instantly to the very direct question. His mouth thinned, his nostrils flared, his eyes grew chilly. "If that were the case," he explained bluntly, "I could get that itch scratched anywhere. There'd be no need to go sniffin' after someone else's claim."

He got up from the overstuffed chair he was sitting in and walked a few quick steps to the fireplace, draping one arm over the stone mantel, staring down at the empty grate.

"So," Drew Buchanan stated matter-of-factly in his rumbling baritone, his eyes focused on Burke, "you're in love with big brother Clay's girl."

Burke nodded, not bothering to raise his head.

"I'd say that you've got a helluva problem then."

"No kidding," Burke responded sardonically.

"Does the lady know how you feel about her?"

"Not a clue." He slanted his head to the left, fixing his dark eyes on his sibling. "How could I tell her? What the hell was I supposed to say? Oh, by the way, Ms. Cantrell, while you're considering my brother's proposal, why don't you think about this as well—I'm falling in love with you." Burke sighed. "Yeah, that would have been real smooth."

Drew shifted one long, jean-clad leg across the opposite knee. He stretched out both arms across the back of the sofa in the den. "It would have at least been honest."

"For me, perhaps." Burke knew honesty came with a price. "But it wouldn't have been fair, to her or to Clay."

"How long's it been since you've seen or talked to her?"

"Three weeks." Damn, Burke thought, it felt more like three years. He could still smell the scent of her perfume, feel the softness of her skin when he'd kissed her cheek, recapture the warmth of her hand in his.

"And you still think about her?"

"Every day and, more importantly," Burke stated, his voice raw with longing, "every night."

"So, as far as you know, they're not officially engaged or anything yet, are they?" Drew asked.

"No. Clay told me that Emma wanted time to think about his marriage proposal. She was to give him his answer New Year's Eve."

Drew ran one large hand through his dark hair. It was the same shade as Burke's, a deep sable brown, though worn longer, touching the back of his neck. It had a curl to it and one thick, waving strand fell languidly across Drew's wide forehead. "Are they lovers?"

Burke shook his head.

Drew arched his dark brows in surprise. "They're not?" His incredulity was evident in his tone. "Damn, Clay must be losing his touch."

"Give it a rest, Drew," Burke snapped.

"Sorry, little brother. It's just that sex is a vital part of life, of relationships."

"Obviously not all relationships."

"Granted, one does have to be cautious these days," Drew admitted. "But it's a basic, natural function. And if, like you said, they've been dating for over six months, I would have thought they would have slept together by now, if for no other reason than propinquity." Drew stood up to his full height. He was about four inches taller than Burke and slightly broader in the chest and shoulders. He wore a cream-colored, Irish hand-knit sweater he'd picked up in a small town in County Cork while on an assignment there several months ago.

"They haven't," Burke repeated.

"Then I would see that as a good sign for you," Drew offered.

"How so?"

"If they're not having a sexual relationship, then there's hope that whatever they feel for one another isn't as deep as it should be, otherwise why not take it to the next level and see how compatible they are in bed?"

"So, you wouldn't consider marrying anyone you hadn't slept with?" Burke asked, his curiosity roused by his older brother's observations.

Drew shrugged his shoulders, replying honestly, "I doubt it. Why would I?"

Burke stared at him, the silence stretching.

"What?" Drew asked.

"Nothing."

"Sorry, little brother," Drew declared, "I don't buy that. Something's up. What?"

Burke threw him a quizzical glance. "I was just wondering if you've ever been in love."

"Not really. In lust lots of times," he frankly admitted. "But what you're describing? Not yet." His deep brown eyes, another trait he shared with Burke, were thoughtful. "I might have thought I was when I was younger. In college there was a girl I could have loved, maybe."

"What happened?"

"We dated for a while, and when it started getting heavy, I wasn't sure I was ready to take it further, especially when she said that she wanted to get married right away and have kids."

"And you didn't."

"That's right. I didn't have it in me then to do what she planned. I wasn't ready to change my life for a kid and happily ever after. She moved on, and so did I." Drew stepped closer to his brother, throwing one arm about Burke's shoulder, whispering, "But at least we did know that we were good for each other in bed. That part was great."

"It doesn't matter to me if I haven't slept with Emma yet, Drew. I know I love her," Burke said, his deep-voiced, husky declaration a statement of irrefutable fact. "Trouble is, Clay loves her, too."

"And I love you both," Drew admitted, walking back to the sofa and sitting down again.

"I know you do," Burke said. "It wasn't my intention to put you smack in the middle, either. I just needed to talk to someone about this."

"You want my advice?"

Burke gave him a thoughtful glance. "I wouldn't have asked you to come if I didn't."

"Then go for it," Drew advised. "If she's not interested, then isn't it better to know up front rather than wondering what might have been if only you'd acted on your feelings? If this woman's really in love with Clay, then nothing you can say or do, little brother, will shake that love. If she isn't, then it's better that she find out now instead of later, even if what she wants doesn't include you."

Drew paused for a moment, adding, "You've been through the wasted-marriage trip before, Burke. You know firsthand what hell that can be. Look at it this way," he proposed. "You could be saving Clay some future heartache."

Burke clenched and unclenched his left hand several times. "It's easy for you to say 'go for it,' Drew. You're not risking a damned thing."

"That's right," he acknowledged. "I'm not."

"And I would be."

"But wouldn't it all be worth it if you got what you wanted?" Drew questioned. "If the lady reciprocated?" He picked up his nearly empty glass of iced tea from the coffee table. That was one of the things he missed most when traveling—a tall glass of freshly brewed iced tea. No matter what the season or the weather, it was a staple of life on the ranch, or just about anywhere in Texas. "Think about this. You saw them together while they were here. Did she and Clay look like they were in love to you? Did they touch each other, kiss each other, sneak off to be by themselves whenever they could?"

"Clay wasn't here with her all that long before he had to leave," Burke responded.

"That doesn't mean a damned thing and you know it," Drew countered. "Hey, all one has to do is look at our folks to see a man and woman still deeply in love with one another. Or, God knows, Vicky and Joe, for that matter. Did you see anything like that between Clay and this woman?"

Burke considered his brother's words. He recalled Clay's fond glances, his sincere tenderness toward Emma but there had been no hot, searching looks that could scorch the skin—from either of them. Emma hadn't exhibited outward signs of anything other than affection for his brother. She'd been calm and cool, never crossing the boundaries of good taste, never giving a clue as to whether or not she cared about Clay with the same depth that he supposedly loved her.

Burke drew in a deep breath and let it out slowly. "No, I don't think so."

"Then something may be missing. Something vital. The question is, do you think it's worth the risk to find out?" Drew drained the contents of his glass. "There's an old Spanish proverb I remember Grandfather Montenegro quoting. I'm paraphrasing, but it goes something like this: 'Take what you want, said the Lord. Take it and pay for it.' Are you willing to do that, Burke? Are you willing to pay the price that might be demanded?"

Burke sent his brother a penetrating glance. He realized how much he could place at risk by being honest with Emma. His relationship with Clay, for one thing—his eldest brother's respect and love and the closeness they shared. Loss of that would be a bitter price to pay.

Then there was his own considerable pride. To stake that on a mere chance for success, to pin his hope for happiness on a maybe, to offer up his heart on a throw of the dice—could he do it?

It was no good speculating when he already knew the answer.

Burke couldn't give Emma up unless he was forced to. Nor could he put aside the deep feelings she brought out in him. God knows he'd tried these past weeks, tried as hard as he could. Her memory only got stronger with each passing day. She was more and more a part of him, as no one had ever been before. He couldn't pretend that it wasn't so.

"Worst-case scenario is that she turns you down, telling you where to get off," Drew stated. "You might walk away with egg on your face."

"And perhaps a sizable rift in my relationship with Clay?" Burke countered. "Maybe even with our parents?"

"True," Drew agreed. "Either of those is a possibility."

But Emma was worth it, Burke thought. She was worth those risks and more. No matter how slim the chance of success, he had to take action. He had to try. Suppose he did nothing, squandered his one opportunity for lifelong happiness? He had to discover for himself if there was any hope.

After all, wasn't it better to know? Burke could deal with rejection if he had to. He could even deal with the aftermath, should there be one, with his family. But he couldn't go on wondering any longer.

"You're right, Drew," he acknowledged with a sense of purpose. "I can't pretend that I don't have feelings for Emma. What I need to know is if she feels anything for me. If there's something there to explore or build on. If not," he said, "then there's an end to it, once and for all."

"No doubt about it, little brother, you've got guts!" Drew declared. "That's one of the things I've always admired about you. You can make a tough decision and stick with it. Not many people can. And you're honorable, Burke. Not many can lay claim to that trait, either." There was a cynical edge to Drew's voice, the result of years of practicing his trade. "Most men, and a lot of women, would have gone for what they wanted immediately, and damn the consequences."

"Don't give me too much praise."

"I give what you deserve," Drew said. "By the way, between us, how long has it been?"

"How long has what been?" Burke asked.

"Since you've scratched that particular itch. Months? A year or so?"

Burke smiled. "Longer," he replied.

"How long?" Drew persisted, his natural curiosity kicking into overdrive.

The smile left Burke's mouth. "Since Celia."

"No way!" Drew declared, surprise on his face at his brother's honest confession. "You're practically still a virgin."

"Not quite."

"But damn near. That's twelve years, Burke," he said, almost dumbfounded.

In a soft voice, Burke replied, "It was my choice, Drew."

"You chose celibacy willingly? Why?" Drew couldn't imagine making, or for that matter, keeping, such a life-altering decision.

"Honestly?" Burke sat back down on the overstuffed green chair and took a deep breath. "Because after that fiasco with Celia, I vowed I was never going to be such a damned fool again." Cupping his hands together, he brought them to his lips, reflecting for a minute on what he'd just said. "I wasn't ever going to allow any woman to get that close to me, not for a very long time. If ever," he added quietly.

"That changed when you fell in love with Emma, didn't it?"

Burke nodded abruptly. "Yes. I want to be with her, in that way. Hell, in every way. Does that make sense?"

"Yeah," Drew said. "It does. She must be some lady."

Burke smiled. "She is."

"Then when are you planning to make your move? Is Clay still out of town?"

"He's been back and forth between Houston and California with some business project since Thanksgiving. As far as I know, that's still ongoing."

"He hasn't been back here?"

"No." Burke shifted in his chair.

"So, if he's traveling, chances are that he and the artist aren't spending much time together right now."

"I doubt it."

"Hmm. Do you know where she is?"

"Let's say that I think I know where she'll be. This weekend there's a charity function in San Antonio."

"La Navidad de Los Niños?" Drew named their aunt's charity.

"Yes, that's it," Burke said. "Vicky told me Emma was donating a painting to the auction, so I think I'll go there and bid on it." He stood up. "Maybe she'll be there. If not," he vowed, "then I'll track her down if I have to."

Drew grinned at the determined tone in his younger brother's voice. "Go for it."

"Thanks." Burke smiled, his brown eyes gleaming with resolve. "I damn well intend to."

Emma stepped back from the painting, a contented smile on her face.

She was pleased with the results of her weeks of hard work. Her artistic vision had finally connected, and she'd produced a picture she was immeasurably proud of. It was large and detailed, her many hours of meticulous research work paying off handsomely. Emma wanted it to be perfect, a reflection of the spirit of the time and place she meant to convey.

Picking up her mug of coffee, she gave the canvas another critical glance. Bluebonnets and Indian paintbrush dotted the landscape of the Texas Hill Country. It was spring, time for new beginnings. A man and a woman were out for a ride in their elegant buggy, dressed in their Sunday best. The man, seen from the side, had a familiar profile. The woman, her essence captured in a myriad details—a gloved hand, a strand of long auburn hair that had escaped from beneath her bonnet and blew in the breeze, the material of her skirt—was also familiar. Emma saw her in the mirror each day.

Artistic license, she told herself. Personal whimsy.

The couple's ride had been interrupted by a friendly cowhand who drove a small herd of longhorns across their path. He was caught in the act of doffing his hat to the woman as a token of respect to her and as a salute to his employer.

Emma had entitled the painting *The Boss's Lady*.

This was the one she would donate to the charity auction this coming weekend. She hoped it would provide the group's coffers with a plentiful boost, even though she was sorely tempted to keep the work herself.

As of this moment Emma was still unsure as to whether or not to attend the function. There were sure to be Buchanans there, or if not, then certainly some of their relatives. Vicky definitely. Santina possibly.

There was even going to be a fancy, invitation-only dance and informal supper after the auction.

And Clay was still waiting for her answer.

He'd called two days ago to ask her to be his guest at the event. She'd received her own invitation, courtesy of his aunt, two weeks before.

Since coming back from the ranch, Emma had played phone tag with Clay, and when they'd finally connected, she'd kept the conversation on safe topics. She couldn't tell him over the phone what was in her heart; it had to be face-to-face. That was the only fair way to accomplish what she must.

She mulled over his invitation.

It would be the perfect opportunity.

Before she could change her mind, Emma hurried the short distance from her studio to the house. She entered through the kitchen and picked up the extension hanging on the wall, punching out Clay's office number in Houston.

The line was answered by his capable secretary, and Emma was immediately put through.

"Hello, Clay."

"Hello yourself, stranger. God, I feel like it's been forever since I've seen you..." He paused dramatically. "Held you... kissed you..."

Emma wet her lips. Clay must be alone in his office.

Or at least she hoped he was.

"I know," she agreed in a neutral tone. "It's been awhile."

"Much too long, sweetheart."

"Then why don't we remedy that?" she asked, opening her refrigerator and withdrawing a bottle of cold water. She twisted the cap off and drank deeply.

"When?" he asked.

"This weekend," she replied. "I'd be happy to be your guest at the charity party."

"Fine. Do you want me to send the jet to Taos to pick you up? Jim will fly you back here and then we can make it a long weekend. I promise you that I'll clear my calendar," he added with a soft laugh.

"No, don't bother," Emma stated. "I'll meet you in San Antonio."

If he felt any disappointment at her request, he didn't let it show in his voice when he said, "If that's what you want. I just thought it would give us more time together if you came to Houston first and we flew to San Antonio together."

"Normally, I would love to," Emma prevaricated. "But I'll be busy until the moment I leave here."

"Okay. Hold on a minute, will you?" Clay asked. "I've got another call."

Emma took another sip of her water, waiting for Clay to get back to her.

"Emma, are you still there?"

"Right here, Clay."

"Good. Sorry about that, but it couldn't be helped."

"I understand."

"That's one of the things I love about you, Emma."

She swallowed. God, he was making this difficult. She hated the thought of hurting him. Only the knowledge that it would hurt Clay more to marry someone who didn't love him the way he deserved to be loved kept her focused. That, and the mental picture she carried in her head and in her heart of his brother.

"Look, Clay, I've got to go. I didn't plan on keeping you this long."

"That's all right, sweetheart," he said. "We'll have all the time in the world this weekend. We have a house in town, so you won't have to fight for a hotel room. San Antonio gets kinda crowded around Christmastime. Here's the address." Clay rattled it off quickly. "Got that?"

Emma made a note of it on the memo pad next to the phone, but asserted, "I'd rather stay at a hotel, if you don't mind, Clay."

"What for?" he asked, puzzled by her reluctance. "You'll love the house. Very Victorian. It's been in my family for over a hundred years."

"It sounds wonderful, but I think I really would prefer to stay in one of the hotels."

"Well, if you insist."

She tried to put a light note into her voice. "I do, really. Humor me."

"No problem, sweetheart." He gave in gracefully. "Let me know where you're staying. If you want any recommendations, give my mother a call. She'll know the best places."

"Thanks. I'll see you on Saturday night, then." .

"Right. Take care, sweetheart."

Emma hung up, draining the last of the water from the plastic bottle.

She'd set the wheels in motion. In a couple of days she would close the book on this chapter of her life, and in doing so, more than likely lose a good friend in the process.

Emma picked up the phone again and dialed another long-distance number. She heard the click of an answering machine, then its recorded message.

As soon as she heard the beep, she said, "If you're there, Kate, please pick up. I need to talk to you."

"Hold on," a feminine voice said. "What's up?"

"I've decided to tell Clay this weekend that I won't be accepting his proposal."

"Good move," the other woman stated.

"Yes, I took your advice. I couldn't wait any longer."

"Great. It's best to get it over with. No sense prolonging the agony. I can tell that it's been bothering you. This way you can both get on with your lives."

"I hope so."

"Are you still thinking about *him?*"

There was no need for Kate to identify who she meant. "Constantly."

"What do you intend on doing afterward?"

"About what?"

"Hello there," Kate said mockingly. "Who are we talking about? Burke Buchanan."

"Nothing. I told you before why it can't happen between us."

"What you told me before were excuses."

"No, they weren't," Emma said defensively.

"Yes, they bloody well were," Kate retorted, refusing to back down. "Remember who you're talking to, girl."

"A good friend."

"And don't you forget it," she insisted. "Time to get your rear in gear and go for it."

"I can't," Emma declared. "Burke isn't interested."

"How do you know?"

"Because I do."

"You'll never know for sure until you try."

"I know, believe me. Don't you think I would have sensed something?"

"Not necessarily," Kate countered. "Men can keep their feelings very well hidden if they want to. It doesn't mean they don't have them; it's just that they're not as comfortable with them as we are. Besides, from what you told me, Burke wasn't the type of guy to come on to his older brother's girlfriend."

"What about the age difference?"

"Emma, give me a break, would you?" Kate said in exasperation. "You're putting up imaginary road-blocks. What's the big deal in five years?"

"It could be to him."

"You'll never know for sure unless you try, will you?" she countered. "There's no shame in falling in love, Emma. It happens to all of us." Kate's voice grew quieter, more thoughtful. "The only sin is in letting an opportunity for it pass you by when you could have grabbed it. Remember, I know firsthand how little time one can have with a loved one."

"I get your drift, Kate. And I will think about it," Emma promised. "How can I help it? He's been a presence in my life I can't ignore."

They chatted for several more minutes before Emma hung up. She knew her friend made sense. It was just that telling Burke was such a big risk. She had a lot to lose.

She also had a lot to gain.

Emma walked back to her studio, searching for her sketchbook. She flipped through it, studying each drawing, pouring over each detail. It was filled with his image, lovingly drawn. His every mood was brought to life.

One page in particular held her interest. It was a simple pencil sketch done the night of Jessie's birthday.

Emma had captured his smile, and with it, the underlying hint of boyish charm beneath the brooding exterior.

It was a smile that reached his dark eyes and ultimately touched her soul.

She would push aside the consequences, banish the doubts, forget the hesitancy, she decided. Maybe not tomorrow, but soon. After all, she'd already lost her heart to Burke. It was time to see if he was interested in keeping it.

Chapter Thirteen

Emma sipped at her hot tea, enjoying the pleasant strains coming from the antique, gold-inlaid Steinway piano in the famed Peacock Alley of the St. Anthony Hotel in San Antonio. She glanced at her watch as she waited for Clay to show up.

When she'd arrived in town early this morning, she had immediately telephoned the Buchanan house on King William Street. She had left a message with the housekeeper, asking Clay to meet her at her hotel. Neutral territory was best for what she had to impart to him, she'd concluded, especially since she found out that not only were Vicky and Joe staying at the King William house that weekend, but Santina and Noah were there also. It certainly wasn't the place to conduct the personal business she had in mind.

Anxious, Emma nibbled on another of the elegant tea sandwiches, then poured herself another cup of the strong English tea. Having skipped lunch, she was moderately hungry. She could have stayed in her room and ordered room service, but having heard about the afternoon tea served in such exquisite surroundings, she'd decided to try it.

Besides, she found it calming to be sitting there, listening to the music, viewing the elegant, old-world Christmas decorations all around her. A time of joy and harmony, the season to be jolly.

She wondered if she would feel that way after she and Clay had their talk.

So wrapped up was she in her thoughts that she didn't even notice the man heading in her direction. However, plenty of other women in the room gave the tall, handsome man long, lingering glances.

"Emma."

Her head jerked as she heard the familiar masculine voice. "Clay," she responded warmly, putting down her cup. The bone china rattled shakily on the saucer.

"God, but I've missed you like crazy," Clay said in a slightly husky tone, taking the seat closest to her after lightly kissing her mouth in greeting. He stared at her for a few seconds. "Let's go somewhere private so I can show you," he suggested.

Emma wet her lips with the tip of her tongue. "Yes, that would be best," she agreed in a soft voice, rising from her chair. "My room."

Clay took her hand, interlacing his fingers through hers. "Perfect," he said, his mouth quirked in a contented smile.

Several minutes later they entered the well-appointed room Emma had checked into earlier. As soon as the door closed behind them, Clay took Emma in his arms, longing to show her just how much he had missed her.

When she averted her face from his kiss, so that he brushed her pale cheek instead of her lips, Clay raised his head and scrutinized her. "What's wrong?"

Emma deliberately stepped away from him, turning her back while she composed herself. "I told you there was something I wanted to discuss with you."

"Yes, you did, but I had thought that perhaps you might want to show me you're glad to see me," he said, surprised by her apparent coolness. "Or was I wrong?"

Emma forced a small smile to her lips as she turned to face him. "It's difficult for me to say..."

"What's so difficult about a simple question?" he interjected quickly. "Either you missed me, Emma, or you didn't."

"I did, Clay. It's just that..."

"What?"

"It wasn't in the same way."

"Wait a minute," he said, his growing confusion apparent. "What's going on here? Are you upset with me for some reason that I'm not aware of?"

Emma hastened to reassure him. "No, of course not."

"Then what is it?" he asked, puzzled. "It's not like you to be so distant. Are you feeling okay?"

"I'm fine, really."

Clay stood there, a bewildered look on his face. His blue eyes were partially hidden by his gold-framed glasses. Carefully, he removed them, setting them inside their monogrammed, brown leather carrying case and placing it back in the interior pocket of his gray wool jacket.

Emma watched him, thinking that Clay was every inch the dynamic, successful businessman, from the top of his well-groomed head to the soles of his expensive, handmade Italian shoes. A man any woman would want to have, both on her arm and in her arms.

"I don't think you're telling me the truth, Emma." He stepped closer, reaching out his hand to her.

"You're right," she conceded at last, moving away from him once again. She sank down on the nearby sofa, patting the seat next to her. "Please."

Clay walked over and joined her, leaving a small space between them. "Okay. Now be straight with me. What's wrong? When I got your message I thought that you'd be happy to see me. That you *wanted* to see me."

"I do, actually. It's just that this is so hard for me to say."

"What's so hard?" He paused, fixing her with a demanding glance. A slow realization dawned on him. "Is it about my marriage proposal?"

"Yes."

"Then you've made up your mind?"

Emma took a deep breath. "I have."

Clay took his eyes from her face, staring down at the expensive carpet, as if it contained the answer he wanted. He had a sinking feeling that he wasn't going to like what she had to say. Clay wasn't stupid. He'd known that something was wrong the moment he saw her. Instead of the usually smiling, happy Emma, the woman who could light up a room just by walking into it, there was an element of sadness about her. As if she'd lost something—or someone. When he'd moved to kiss her, the quick movement of her head so that their lips wouldn't meet had been like an outright slap to his masculine ego. She'd turned away so that he wasn't able to fully demonstrate to her just how much he'd missed being with her this past month.

"And?" he insisted.

"I want you to know just how much your proposal meant to me, Clay. I was flattered. Incredibly so. Maybe more than you know." Her pale, blue-green eyes met his and their glances locked. "For so long my career was the true love of my life," she explained, trying to put her feelings into words. "I put all my energy into it, building my name and my reputation. It was what I wanted, at the time.

"Then, I met you," she said softly.

Emma flashed him a genuine smile, her eyes warm with affection. "With you, I discovered another part to my life. A part that I was ready to share with someone. You helped me to see that there were other possibilities I had conveniently ignored. For that I'm grateful."

Clay stated honestly, "It's not your gratitude I want."

"I know that," Emma acknowledged "You want what you deserve—a woman who loves you as much and as best she can. I want that for you, too." She could see in his eyes the dawning recognition of what she was saying. "Unfortunately, I've come to the conclusion that it's just not me."

"If you don't mind my asking, what led you to this sudden conclusion?" Clay queried in a very calm voice.

"A number of things."

"Such as?"

Emma lowered her lashes, breaking the contact between them. *Falling in love with your brother, Burke,* was the answer that popped immediately to her mind. However, it was the one answer she couldn't give him. What could she say that wouldn't sound false?

"You're stalling, Emma," he said quietly. "Believe it or not, I'm a big boy now. I can take it."

She focused her gaze on him once more. "I realized that I wasn't in love with you."

Clay absorbed this news. "How did you reach that conclusion?"

"As I said before, a number of different things," she reiterated. "I can't put my finger on just one."

"Why don't I believe you?"

"I don't know," she said.

Afraid that he would read the truth in her eyes, Emma averted her glance, focusing instead on her hands, staring at the ring on her little finger that Burke's grandmother had given her on Thanksgiving. It brought back to her mind that time spent with Burke, sweet hours of delight laced with the bittersweet knowledge that it was all fleeting.

"Is there someone else?" His softly spoken question invaded her thoughts.

Emma believed that she owed Clay honesty, even if it was an abridged version. But what was the whole truth? Yes, there was another man. But no, he didn't love her, so he wasn't even part of the equation.

"That doesn't really matter."

Clay was adamant. "I should damn well think it does," he stated. "I didn't even know you were interested in someone else."

"I wasn't." That, at least, was a part of the truth. Emma hadn't been interested in anyone else when she began dating Clay.

"But in these past few weeks you've met another man, haven't you?"

"Would it really matter if I had?"

"Yes," he answered. "I'd like to know about the competition. What can he offer you that I can't?"

"Nothing," she said sadly.

"I don't get it then." Clay looked around the room, anywhere but at her face. Silence hung between them for several minutes before he broke the hold it had on them with his next question. "Who is he?"

Emma responded, "A satisfied customer." It was another small part of the truth, she knew. Burke had loved her painting.

"Have you known him long?"

"No."

Clay's eyes were riveted once more on her face. "So this happened quickly?"

"Yes."

"Are you in love with him?"

"Yes," she answered simply.

"Does he love you?"

"No." It hurt Emma to say the word out loud.

"Did you sleep with him?" His pride forced him to ask the question. He regretted it as soon as it left his mouth.

Would that I had, Emma thought. I could have held those memories close.

"No."

"Let me get this straight," he said. "You're telling me that you're turning me down for a man who doesn't love you?"

Emma swallowed the lump that rose in her throat. "Not for him, Clay, for you." She saw the look of disbelief that came over his features at that remark. "You have to know that I care about you, deeply."

"But not enough to marry, right?"

"I would do you a great disservice if I did," she replied honestly.

"Because you love him." It was a flat statement.

"Yes. And because, in loving him, I found out that what I feel for you *is* love, just not the right kind of love."

Perversely, Clay had to know. "What kind is it?"

Emma struggled to put it into words that would soften the impact. "The type that one friend feels for another."

"A friend," he repeated.

"Yes."

"You're sure?"

"Very."

"Then I suppose that's it." Clay rose.

Emma did also. "I wish that . . ."

"What? That you didn't love him?"

"No. I can't regret what I feel for him," she admitted. "I just wish that..." She paused, trying to come up with a new way to say a clichéd phrase. But she couldn't think of any other way to say it. "I wish that we could remain friends."

Clay stared at her. *"Friends,"* he said bitingly. "How charming. Let me think on it, will you?" He strode to the door.

Emma followed. "I'm sorry, Clay. I never meant to hurt you, really." She stretched out her hand and touched the sleeve of his jacket. She could instantly feel the tensing of his muscles beneath the material.

Reluctantly, she let go.

Clay kept his back to her, one hand on the doorknob. "No, Emma," he acknowledged sadly, "I don't suppose that you did."

He opened the door and shut it behind him.

Emma stood at the door, her forehead leaning against the wood for a few minutes. Selfishly, she knew that she'd miss him. Selfishly, she wanted to call him back, to try and make him see the situation differently.

However, she couldn't. Dragging it out would only prolong the inevitable conclusion. Things wouldn't change. There would still be questions unanswered.

Emma pulled a linen handkerchief from the pocket of her slacks, dabbing at her eyes, drying her wet lashes.

Some secrets weren't meant to be shared. This was one of them.

Burke's Jeep Wagoneer sped along the highway, heading toward San Antonio. Haunting strains of classical music filled the car as the female cellist perfectly captured the sensual mood of a Vivaldi concerto.

Burke stared at the road in front of him, mechanically driving while his thoughts focused on the reason for his trip. He'd made up his mind that morning, having awakened once more from a dream that left him craving the reality instead of the fantasy.

Emma. Everything these days, for him, came back to Emma. Like a thorn imbedded so deeply into his flesh as to become a grafted part of his skin, she was there.

On the off chance that she would attend the charity auction tonight, Burke had decided to go. He kept that news to himself, not wanting to alert his family to his sudden interest in this function. His arrival at the hotel hosting the event would be signal enough of his interest and involvement.

If Emma didn't come, Burke still intended to bid on whatever painting she had donated. His checkbook, along with his embossed invitation, rested securely in the inside pocket of his black, Western-style dinner jacket. He was determined that no one would outbid him tonight.

And what if Emma was there, as he hoped?

And suppose that big brother Clay was with her? What then?

Burke's wide mouth twisted in a half smile. He'd deal with that eventuality if and when he had to. Nothing and no one was going to stop him. His mind was made up.

"There's nothing to be nervous about," Vicky declared as she came up to Emma, who stood on one side of the room where the charity auction was taking place.

"Easy for you to say," Emma retorted, trying hard to keep her focus on the events unfolding instead of on the up-tempo beating of her heart. Her painting would soon be on the block.

"You've got nothing to worry about, you know," Vicky insisted. "I overheard several people discussing it, and I predict that you'll be real pleased with the outcome of the bid."

"I just hope your aunt is pleased."

"She's in her element right now."

"Ladies?" A male voice interrupted. A handsome waiter held out a silver tray holding fluted champagne glasses.

Emma and Vicky each helped themselves to a glass, and he moved on.

Emma wished that she was drinking a cold bottle of beer instead, but she sipped at the sparkling vintage just the same.

"I saw Clay today," Vicky said between sips. "He seemed in some kind of a funky mood. Do you know anything about it?"

Emma glanced quickly at the other woman. "Is he here?"

"No." Vicky waved to a couple entering the room. "He left the house and went back to Houston. Which was kind of strange, since when he arrived this morning he said that he was planning on staying for the entire weekend.''

''I guess there's no reason for you not to know now,'' Emma began, pausing to take another taste of the champagne. ''We broke up.''

''Damn,'' Vicky said, disappointed. ''I'm sorry.''

''Don't be,'' Emma murmured. ''It's for the best.''

''I like you, Emma. I was sort of hoping that we'd be family one day.''

''And I like you, Vicky, along with your entire family.''

''So let's not let this put a dent in our friendship then,'' the other woman suggested.

''I'd like that,'' Emma agreed.

''Still, I honestly do wish that things could have been different.''

''Clay's a good man,'' Emma stated. ''We just weren't meant to be, I'm afraid.''

Vicky shrugged her bare shoulders. ''I guess it's better that you decide this now rather than after you two were married.''

''Yes, it is.''

They stood there watching the next item come up for bid. It was a piece of Joe's handcrafted furniture.

''If you'll excuse me,'' Vicky said, her dark eyes filled with love and pride for her lover's excellent craftsmanship, ''I want to be with Joe.''

''Go ahead,'' Emma said.

''Why don't you join us when this is over?''

''I'll think about it.''

''Good. Do that. I'll see you later then,'' Vicky whispered as she made her way down the aisle to the empty seat next to Joe.

Emma smiled from her vantage point in the back of the room when his work went for a high price.

Her painting was next.

She drained the contents of her glass and replaced it with another when the same waiter came back around. Emma heard the amplified voice of Santina Buchanan's sister as she described the item now up for bid.

"We've very lucky to have one of this country's top artists represented tonight. It's the first showing of her work in this event, but I'm sure it's not the first time that her artistry has been seen by most of you here this evening."

The painting was brought onto the stage and ceremoniously unveiled amidst excited applause from the crowd. "Inspired, the artist says, by a recent trip to the Encantadora ranch, of which I have a passing acquaintance—" the last line drew quite a few laughs from about the room "—this is a slice of Texas's colorful past interpreted with a modern eye. The title is *The Boss's Lady*." She wielded her gavel. "Now, what am I bid?"

Emma held her breath while the auction started. Someone opened at ten thousand, causing her to sigh in relief, and the amount climbed steadily upward.

When it reached as high as she thought it would go, which was more than she had ever imagined, there was another bid—for fifty thousand.

Emma gasped, the Waterford champagne glass almost slipping from her fingers. She rescued it just in time to avert an embarrassing accident.

A painful breath caught in her chest as her heart skipped a beat. She recognized that decidedly masculine voice.

Burke.

She must be hallucinating. It couldn't be him. What in the world would he be doing here? It had to be a trick of her overheated imagination.

"Going once. Twice." Emma heard the auctioneer's voice pause, as if waiting for another bid.

When none ensued, she said, "Sold then to Mr. Burke Buchanan for fifty thousand dollars."

God, it was him, Emma discovered. He was actually here.

Why?

Burke stepped forward from his position in the back of the room. As of yet, he hadn't seen Emma. All he knew was that he'd almost lost his chance to bid on the painting. He'd been waylaid by an old friend in the lobby, who insisted that Burke just had to meet someone in his party.

Burke tried to beg off politely, but his friend wouldn't take no for an answer, so he reluctantly agreed, insisting that he could stay only a few minutes at best.

Five minutes turned into fifteen, then twenty before he finally got away. When he entered the ballroom, he heard the bidding and quickly checked the catalogue he'd been handed. Emma's painting was up for grabs, and he was determined that no one would have it but him, no matter what it cost.

When, after a series of increments, the bid climbed to thirty-five thousand, Burke decided he was through playing this game and he set his bid.

He heard the surprised gasps. He even saw Vicky turn around in her seat to see who had made what would be the final offer. The look on his cousin's face was utterly priceless when she recognized the purchaser.

Burke was beyond caring what anyone thought about his motives.

"On behalf of *La Navidad de Los Niños,* I want to express our thanks for such a generous gesture." His aunt led the assembly in a heartfelt round of applause.

Burke nodded his dark head briefly in acknowledgment.

"And," she continued, "I want to thank the artist herself, who is here with us tonight." She brought her hands together again.

Burke quickly scanned the room, searching for Emma. At last he spied her, standing to his left. Without hesitation, he strode toward her.

She was beautiful, he thought as he approached. Standing there, she looked like the answer to his most fervent prayer. Her shapely form was clothed in a simple black velvet suit that accentuated all her curves, the skirt ending just an inch or so above her knees. With the suit she wore a blouse of apricot silk. his gaze dropped down her black-stockinged legs to the modest, black velvet heels. The delightfully feminine package stirred him instantly.

Like a match to dry wood, Burke could feel the heat rising in his body, ready to blaze higher, stronger, hotter than ever before. All for this woman.

"Emma."

He could read the astonishment in her blue-green eyes, so like the color of an aquamarine.

"Hello, Burke," she said, her words coming out in a husky murmur. "I didn't expect to see you here."

"Then we're even."

"We are?"

"Yes," he said with a deepening smile. "I wasn't certain you would come tonight, either."

Emma didn't quite know how to respond to that comment. "Actually, I didn't know myself till almost the last minute," she admitted. She wet her lips, drawing Burke's attention to the fullness of them and the dark wine color of the lipstick she used. "I must admit I'm flattered that you thought so much of my work to make that very generous bid. What a lovely compliment."

He had to ask the next question. "Where's Clay?"

Emma met his gaze. "He isn't here tonight."

"Now it's my turn to be surprised. I would have thought my big brother would have made an effort to be here for this, for you."

"He was."

"Was?" Burke raised one curving dark brow. "What happened?"

Emma was frank. "Clay decided to go back to Houston."

"Did you two have an argument?"

"Not exactly."

Burke could tell that something wasn't right. It was evident in the tone of Emma's voice. He could see it in her face.

He couldn't deny the fact that he was selfishly glad that Clay had left. If big brother could willingly walk away from this woman, then he was a fool who didn't deserve her.

"Do you prefer not to talk about it?" he asked.

Emma replied, "I don't know what to say."

"Because I'm Clay's brother?"

A ghost of a smile crossed her mouth. "Sort of."

"Maybe I can help," he offered. "Forget that fact and pretend I'm just a friend."

"Considering that your last name is the same as Clay's and that you just spent fifty thousand dollars on one of my paintings, I'd say that would take some real acting ability."

"I'm willing if you are," Burke proposed.

He could see that she was considering his offer. "All right."

"Then let's get out of here," he suggested. "I know that a fancy dinner goes along with this deal, but—"

"Would you mind if we skipped it?" she asked. "I'd rather go someplace a little more quiet."

"No," he said, smiling. "How do you feel about Mexican?"

"Fajitas?"

"Whatever you want."

"Okay."

"Let me go and get my car," he said. "I'll meet you out front in a couple of minutes."

Emma watched Burke as he left the room.

Had she just made a big mistake?

Recklessly, she'd thrown aside any qualms, pushed behind her all the nagging doubts. Time enough for them later. Right now she wanted to grab this moment and hold on for as long as she could.

Tonight, when she'd needed him, Burke was there. Conjured up like a magician's trick, or better still, like a fantasy come to life. Hopefully, that meant something in the grand scheme of things.

It might be crazy.

It might be foolish.

It might be asking for trouble.

Right now, Emma didn't care. It was what she wanted. It was what she needed. It was what she had to have.

She would play it as it came.

Chapter Fourteen

It was playing well so far, Emma thought.

She and Burke were sitting at a small, intimate table in a restaurant along the River Walk. They'd been there for more than two and a half hours, eating, talking and generally getting to know one another better.

A candle burned low in the dark blue glass holder, pushed to one side so that there was nothing between them on the table. Music played in the background. It was soft and flavored with a Latin rhythm.

Emma and Burke had avoided the subject of Clay Buchanan. They'd kept to neutral topics, the kind of things people discussed when they were first dating.

Emma realized that that notion was absurd. This wasn't a real date. It was actually...

What? she asked herself. Merely a simple meal, no strings, no promises.

Still, she fancied the idea of this evening as the beginning of a courtship. Such an old-fashioned word that brought with it sweet thoughts.

Reality, however, intruded with a blunt edge. Emma knew that she would soon have to say something about her situation with Clay. After all, that was supposedly the purpose of this dinner—to talk about the fact that Clay had returned to Houston, alone. Still, she didn't want to spoil the amicable mood.

"Would you like dessert?"

Seizing on any opportunity to linger with him awhile longer, Emma decided that she did, in spite of the fact that dinner had been quite filling. "Yes," she answered with enthusiasm.

Burke summoned the rotund woman who'd greeted them when they first entered the restaurant. She was hostess, occasional waitress and along with her husband, the chef, owner of this place. *La Rosa del Norte* was a haven from the artificial and the overpriced in San Antonio. Here they served good food at reasonable prices, with excellent service in a comfortable atmosphere.

It had the kind of relaxed ambiance Emma preferred. Four-star establishments were nice, but for her, they weren't real. She'd liked Burke's choice immediately. It was a place conducive to kicking back. So she had.

The woman made her way to their table, a wide smile on her round face, her dark eyes bright with delight. "Ah, Senor Buchanan, is there something else I can do for you and the lovely lady?"

"Some of your excellent coffee, for starters," Burke ordered in a low voice. "And what do you have for dessert tonight?"

The woman gave a throaty laugh. "A chocolate cake fit for the angels," she promised.

Burke threw Emma a glance.

"That sounds wonderful," she agreed.

"Good," he said. He addressed the owner. "We'll have two."

"Let me get your plates out of the way," Rosa said, bending to scoop up the discarded items, "and I'll see to it personally."

She was back in a minute with two steaming cups of freshly brewed coffee and a jug of warm milk. Clearing the rest of the table, she walked away again, humming a Spanish love song beneath her breath.

A few minutes later she hurried back to their table. "Here it is," she said a second later with a deep chuckle. "Eat it if you dare."

"I wonder what she meant by that?" Emma asked when Rosa had once again left them alone.

Burke looked at the large slices of cake, at the thick layers of frosting, the whipped cream, the flecks of white chocolate in the cake itself, and sighed. "I would guess that if you can finish this, you are a certified chocolate addict. Or perhaps," he suggested with a raised brow, his voice pitched to a low, intimate tone, "if you eat every last bite, you may expire from sheer pleasure."

"I'm game then," Emma quipped, sinking her fork into the confection. The idea of expiring from pleasure brought another scene to her mind, and it had nothing to do with eating cake.

She sighed in delight after her first taste. "Heaven. Or the devil's temptation," she said wryly. "I'm going to have to exercise my buns off to get rid of the calories."

Burke leveled a glance at his companion noting with satisfaction the way her silk blouse dipped into a V, re-

vealing a hint of her high, firm breasts. He loved the fact
that Emma looked like a woman, not a half-starved waif
that a good Texas wind would blow into Louisiana. To
him, her figure was ideal. She had curves his hand ached
to hold.

He watched her as she ate, enjoying the way she savored each bite. He almost groaned out loud when she
licked a glob of frosting from her fork, so intense was his
unspoken wish for her to do the same to him. Like a little girl, or a grown-up sensualist, she closed her eyes in
rapture at the flavor, making him long to taste her mouth
right then.

Emma finally put down her fork and picked up her
coffee cup. She wouldn't sleep tonight anyway.

And what's more, she didn't care.

Not tonight.

Not now.

Her insides slowly melted as she glanced at Burke
eating his portion of the dessert. Occasionally, as he
lifted the fork to his mouth, his eyes would meet hers
across the table and she could feel herself falling deeper
and deeper under his spell. It was as if the cake's main
ingredient were tinged with a secret formula that
heightened the senses, warmed the blood.

"What's so funny?" Burke asked.

Emma hadn't realized that she'd laughed out loud,
albeit softly. "Nothing, really."

His dark brown eyes held hers. "So you don't want to
share?"

"It's just a silly thought that crossed my mind, nothing more."

"If you say so."

"I do," she insisted with a smile.

He put aside his fork and gazed at her, wanting so much to touch her skin, to feel the softness of her hair. "I told you earlier this evening that I wanted you to consider me your friend, Emma."

"I try to."

"Fine. Because if you do, then I think it's time to tell me why my brother went back to Houston, alone."

"He wasn't happy with the answer I gave him."

Burke's pulse quickened. Could it be that she had rejected Clay's marriage proposal? And if so, why? Clay wasn't expecting her answer until New Year's Eve.

"Which was?" he asked softly. "If you don't mind my asking."

"I told your brother no."

Burke digested this information. "You must have had a good reason then."

Emma was taken aback by his comment. She'd expected Burke to be angry. To be royally upset that she had rejected his brother. "I did." *You.* The word echoed silently in her brain. *I rejected him for you.*

She took another sip of the coffee. Her mouth was suddenly dry. "Clay is a man in a million, and I'm well aware that he's quite a catch, so to speak. He would be even if he weren't a member of the illustrious Buchanan family."

"But?" Burke prodded.

"As truly fond of your brother as I am," Emma stated, "I'm not in love with him."

"That wouldn't stop a lot of women," Burke observed cynically.

"It would me," she said quietly.

"Clay must have been very upset," he guessed.

"He was more surprised, I think," she said. "Once he's had a chance to think things through, he'll see that

I was right in my decision. Clay deserves a woman who loves him as deeply as he is capable of loving. Anything else would be a joke of the cruelest sort.''

"Then you do care about him?"

"Of course I do, Burke. Very much," Emma assured him.

He couldn't tamp down or deny the joy that flooded through him when she explained her actions. Clay was officially out of her life. While Burke was sorry that his brother was hurting—and he was sure Clay was—he was honest enough to admit that here was his golden opportunity. Life was handing him his dream and challenging him to take it.

He couldn't refuse.

But he would have to go slowly. Woo her gently and carefully, keeping his deeper feelings in tight check until the right moment. His hungry eyes and oh-so-hungry heart would have to wait. There was no sense in spooking her, and he might if he showed too soon just how much he wanted a closer relationship with her.

He had to give her time to adjust. To accept the possibility that another of the Buchanan men was interested in marrying her.

He was so quiet, Emma observed. Along with being remarkably calm. Had she unwittingly blown this chance to be friends with him? Behind those dark eyes was hidden the truth.

She broke the silence. "You believe me, don't you?"

Brown eyes met blue-green. "Yes."

"I'm glad," she responded.

Burke couldn't resist asking, "My opinion matters that much to you?"

Emma wondered how to answer that. "Yes, it does," she admitted. "As I told Vicky, I like your family a lot.

I don't want anyone, you included, to think that I was not giving Clay's proposal the consideration it deserved, or that I was using him in some way."

"From what I've observed, you're too honest for that," Burke said.

Honest! Her mind screamed the word. If she was honest, Emma thought, she would confess right now that she longed for Burke to kiss her, to gather her tightly in his arms and tell her he never intended to let her go.

Honest? Coming from Burke, that was a compliment of the highest rank. "Thanks, that's nice of you to say."

"I didn't say it to be nice," he admitted. "I believe it to be true."

Suddenly, the walls of the restaurant seemed to be closing in on her. She needed air, some space. Distance from the man. She was too close and was being drawn nearer and nearer, dangerously so. It wouldn't take much to surrender to the almost overwhelming urge to slip that black wool jacket from his shoulders, to pull apart the pearl snaps of his fancy shirt, exposing his long torso. Was he wearing the gold bracelet? She couldn't tell, since the cuffs of his shirt hid the fact.

The intensity of emotion she was experiencing now was the reason she hadn't ever slept with a man before. This was what she'd waited for. This was what she'd dreamed about.

Now it was right in front of her—and she couldn't have it. Like the apple in the Garden of Eden, she wanted to taste the fruit and experience the burning knowledge of love and desire.

But she couldn't stand to see the scorn in Burke's eyes or the rejection in his voice if she were to offer anything beyond the parameters of friendship. Such a gesture might condemn her in his mind, and she couldn't risk that.

No, it was better to retreat while she was able. Regroup later in private. Without Burke nearby, she would be stronger, more in control.

Emma forced herself to check her watch. "It's getting late," she said, managing to keep her voice remarkably calm under the circumstances. God, it was harder and harder to keep up the pretense of viewing him only as a friend.

Burke stated, "I'll settle the bill and drive you back to your hotel." He pushed back his chair and rose.

As soon as he was gone from the table, Emma let out a deep sigh. Every second with him was pleasurable agony. Holding back her true feelings was slowly killing her inside.

"All set," he said when he returned. He held her chair while she stood. "Let's go then."

Burke felt like he was bringing Cinderella home from the ball. Be in before midnight or she was liable to turn into...what? A sharp-tongued user like Celia? Never. This was Emma, the woman who knew what she wanted; her career and love. She had the former and was looking for the latter. His brother hadn't proved to be the prince of her heart. What made him think that he could?

He was no knight in shining armor. Never had been. Never would be, he reckoned. He was simply a man. And as a man, he wanted her—to cherish, to live with, to stand beside, to lie with.

He pulled the car up to the front entrance of the hotel and handed the keys to the waiting valet.

Emma offered a weak objection. "You don't have to come in if you'd rather not."

"No trouble," Burke assured her, escorting her into the lobby. "My mama always told me to see a lady to her door, not to drop her off on the curb."

He was torn between his love for her and his concern for his brother. How was Clay taking the news that Emma wouldn't marry him? Burke certainly knew how he'd feel. Distraught. Confused. Angry. Hurt.

Now, as he stood so close to her that the smell of her perfume was like a shot of adrenaline in his bloodstream, Burke felt desire riding roughshod through him. There was nothing morally to stop him now if he wanted to make his feelings known.

But how would Emma react if he did?

Emma laughed nervously, glancing around as they waited for the elevator. "This is hardly the same thing," she murmured.

"Nevertheless," he said, "I intend to see you to your room. While in Texas, do as we Texans do."

There was a lot to be said for old-world manners, Emma thought as they entered the already occupied elevator. On one hand, she loved the personal attention from Burke. On the other, it would take minutes longer to make her escape. She savored the closeness to be found in his company, even though she knew she had passed into the danger zone with him.

What was wrong with her?

There was nothing to stop her from revealing to him the hidden depths of her emotions. Nothing save wondering how he would react.

They walked down the corridor until they reached her room. Burke took the key from her hand. "Let me," he insisted, slipping it into the lock. He entered first, flipping on the light switch and giving the room a quick, cursory glance. Everything appeared normal.

His gaze fell upon the long-sleeved nightshirt that lay on the bed. It was nothing fancy, just a practical garment that probably ended mid-thigh. It was the shade of rich cream, with a yellow rose embroidered on the pocket.

Burke imagined her wearing it. He took his flight of fancy one step further, imagining his hand deftly making quick work of the fabric-covered buttons, then slipping inside to cup the warm weight of her breast.

What he didn't need to imagine was the stirring reaction of his body to that thought. It was decidedly real.

Embarrassed, Emma grabbed at the garment and flung it into the drawer of the combination dresser-entertainment center. Her heart was racing, its tempo beating faster as she fantasized about Burke's hands on the material of the nightshirt, smoothing, shaping, sweeping over her body in a powerful caress. Those hands, those lips, those eyes, all stripping her bare...

Heat rose in her cheeks. Warmth pooled inside her. Her nipples stiffened against the silky fabric of her bra.

"Everything seems all right," Burke said, his voice a hoarse rasp.

"It was sweet of you to check," she said, moving past him to open the door of her suddenly too small room. He was dominating the space without trying. He had to leave, now. Her senses silently screamed for him, begged for him, ached for him.

Emma stood there, her hand on the brass doorknob. "Thanks for dinner. It was lovely."

"No," he said, contradicting her. "You're what's lovely, Emma."

Please! she thought desperately. *You've got to go. Now.* Before she read too much into his words. Down that path lay the dark danger of unbridled desire.

Burke walked slowly toward her, and when he reached her side, he stopped. He looked down just as she looked up.

Their gazes locked.

He reached out one hand and lifted her chin, tilting it to meet his descending mouth.

It was a sweet, gentle kiss, over far too quickly.

He raised his head.

"Goodbye," she said, her own voice a husky whisper, betraying her tattered emotions.

"*Vaya con Dios,*" Burke whispered in response.

The sound of softly uttered Spanish coming from his mouth, in that sexy, deep baritone, made Emma quiver.

He reacted. Instead of leaving, he reached out and shut the door with a definite click.

Emma's eyes flew open in shocked surprise.

Burke acted on pure instinct, responding to her, to what he was feeling. He couldn't leave her. Not without sharing the emotions that caught him up in the whirlpool they created.

What happened to slow? To caution? To waiting? he asked himself. He shoved them ruthlessly aside in his quest for the moment. Something told him it was now or never.

Burke drew Emma into his arms, his mouth capturing hers. He could feel her initial shock. Then her lips opened to his as her arms rose, creeping slowly up the back of his jacket, pulling him closer.

He had her up against the door, moving nearer, so that there was no space between them.

This was his reality. Here and now. What he wanted. What he'd longed for.

A kiss wasn't just a kiss. It was a glimpse of heaven to come—of just how much he'd missed, of how much he had to learn.

Burke pulled back. He stared down at Emma's flushed face. She was beautiful. Sweet. Powerful in her own right. Woman. He wanted to hold her forever. She was light in the darkness. Shelter from the storm. A rainbow of colors in an otherwise dull, prosaic world.

Tunneling his hands into her auburn curls, he dipped his head again to savor her waiting lips.

It was like no kiss she'd ever known. It spun her mind out of control. She couldn't resist the power of his mouth, the warmth and strength that enveloped her.

What had been beyond her reach was now within her arms.

Emma reveled in the sensations, letting him lead until she had to race to keep up, surrendering to the new beauty.

And it was beautiful. Just as she knew it could be.

A shower of colors, at once brilliant and dramatic, exploded in her brain—blinding white, brilliant blue, shimmering green, dazzling red, magnificent purple. Primal. Basic. Bejeweled.

Her hands, freed of restraint, went to work on the Western-style black wool jacket he wore. She eased open the buttons, shoving it off his broad shoulders as she sought the shirt beneath. Inexperience didn't matter. Instinct took over, giving Emma the confidence to proceed as she would.

There was heat beneath her fingertips. She could feel it as she skimmed her hands over the wide expanse of his lean, muscled chest, then around his waist, drawing him closer.

"Love me," she whispered.

Chapter Fifteen

Emma hadn't realized she had spoken the words out loud until she heard the raw, silky whisper of Burke's voice.

"I intend to," he responded, bending down to scoop her up into his arms. He carried her the short distance to the bed, then set her on her feet beside it. With surprisingly deft fingers, he undid the single button on her velvet jacket. Slowly, he slipped it off her shoulders.

The blood pumped hotly in his veins. It had been so long for him. Years of sexual restraint. This, and the knowledge that there hadn't been anyone for Emma before him, made Burke slightly anxious.

There's no rush, he kept telling himself. Take it slow and steady.

But what if she changed her mind? he wondered. What then?

He pushed that thought aside as Emma stepped out of the shoes she wore. The top of her head came to just below his shoulders. Could she hear the excited tattoo of his heart?

He shucked his own black evening jacket, letting it fall to the floor. He saw the glimmer of sexual arousal in her pale, aquamarine eyes as he tore off his black string tie.

Emma sucked in her breath. Hesitating for only a few seconds, she finally gave in to the overwhelming need to touch Burke. Resting her palms on his chest, she let them linger there for a moment before, acting on gut instinct, she unsnapped the pearl buttons that held his crisp white shirt together, exposing the solid, smooth chest beneath. Like a pagan statue of old, Burke was lean and muscled, his golden skin begging to be touched.

Wetting her lips, Emma did just that, her fingers sliding along the edges of the shirt, pushing it aside, tugging it out of his black trousers. It was like touching live marble, she thought—warm instead of cold, beating with life.

Emma heard Burke's sharp intake of breath when she grazed a hardened male nipple, lingering on that item in her inventory. She explored higher, across the ridge of his collarbone, then back down his long, lean torso, loving the feel of his skin. Her fingertips touched several ridges of puckered flesh near his abdomen. He had several small scars there. It hurt her to think that he'd ever been in any kind of pain.

"My turn now," Burke whispered.

Emma blinked, letting her hands fall limply to her sides. She trembled, waiting for his touch.

When it came, it was soft and gentle. Burke slid the buttons of her apricot silk blouse out of each buttonhole slowly, as if they had years instead of stolen hours.

He drew the material apart, gazing intently at the pale flesh he exposed. His hands made short work of pushing the blouse down her arms and off her body. It landed on the floor atop his jacket.

Emma resisted the urge to shield her arms over her breasts, covered only by a silk-and-lace bra. Instead, she watched Burke watch her. His dark brown eyes looked their fill.

Her nipples puckered in reaction from the heat of his gaze.

He reached out and slid his hands over her skin, around her waist, until he found the button and zipper of her skirt. The velvet garment slid from her hips and pooled on the carpet.

Burke's breath was almost stolen by the sight of Emma clad only in a silky apricot bra and matching tap pants. On her legs were thigh-high black stockings.

He unbuckled the belt he wore, the gold buckle a match to his bracelet, and casually dropped it. He sank to the bed, removing his black dress boots and black socks, never taking his eyes from Emma's face. Then he stood up, drawing back the covers of the bed, exposing the pristine sheet beneath.

He missed her mouth. Now, having tasted the delights to be found there, he couldn't imagine denying himself the experience, and he pulled her back into his embrace.

Emma went willingly.

They clung to each other, skin-to-skin, mouth-to-mouth. Kisses soft and exploring, kisses hard and demanding, kisses meant to succor, kisses that sizzled— they shared them all, finding more and more ways to communicate with their lips.

Emma's fingertips explored Burke's back, learning the play of his muscles as he moved, as he breathed. She loved the texture of his smooth skin. It was warm, undeniably so. Allowing her hands free rein was a dream fulfilled.

It was incredibly liberating to be this close to the man she loved. Wanting to express all she felt for him, Emma set aside any lingering doubts, any lingering questions. She operated purely on emotion, returning every kiss, every caress, until they were both gasping.

It was all so right.

She did what she'd wanted to do since the first day they'd met, winding her arms about Burke's neck, sliding her hands upward to his scalp. His short, sable hair was baby soft.

It was then that Emma felt her feet leave the ground. Burke lifted her high in his arms, never breaking the kiss. Her back came into contact with the sheet.

Then, suddenly, she was alone.

She raised her head from the softness of the pillow to see Burke quickly stripping off his trousers. All that remained were his black cotton shorts. She sighed from the sheer joy of viewing the wonderful symmetry of his body.

"Tell me you want this. That you want *me*," he said thickly, standing there with a questioning look on his face.

That Burke needed her reassurance touched Emma's heart. "Yes," she answered, her voice a murmur of consent, of unquestioning approval. "I want *this*," she stated. She moved, extending her hand in his direction. "I want *you*."

It was all he needed to hear.

Burke joined her on the bed, and Emma welcomed him with her heart, her soul, her body. All she could give was his.

She moaned with delight when his lips began a trail of kisses along her upper body. He took his time, learning all the pleasure points. When he found the sensitive peak of her breast, she gasped with wonder at the sensations he evoked within her. His mouth captured the nipple through the fabric, his tongue laving it.

Seconds later, her bra was gone and Burke's lips replaced the silk.

Her head spun.

It continued doing so when he moved to the other breast, then down her body, placing soft, tender kisses on her flesh.

Burke ran one hand along her stomach, leaving fire in its wake. When he reached her panties and slid one finger beneath the elastic edge, Emma moaned.

With a hint of a smile on his lips, he moved his index finger lower, then slipped the rest of his hand under the silk, exploring. When he reached her soft, auburn curls, Emma felt dizzy from the wonder of it all.

Tipping her head back, she reached out for him, her hands needing to feel him. They met his shoulders, and her nails dug in. Fire leapt in her blood, warming her skin. It was almost more than she could bear. To discover that this man had such power over her, that with just a kiss or caress he could ignite her world, was amazing.

The silk was pushed aside, and down the length of her legs. All that remained were the black, thigh-high stockings.

Burke's lean fingers smoothed through her curls, stoking fires as they slipped inside, finding her damp heat. Satisfied, he captured her mouth once more in another soul-shattering kiss.

Her own hands slid along his back, moving downward to the hard muscles of his buttocks. She ran her fingers over the soft material that clothed him, wanting to remove the last barrier between them. Pushing the cotton down over his hips, she touched the taut warm skin beneath.

Burke broke their kiss to finish what she'd started. "Oh Emma," he said with a groan, "what you do to me! I've never felt like this before. Never. I wish I could put it into words."

"Ssh," she said, gathering him close, feeling the warmth of his bare, sweat-dampened skin on hers, the weight of his body, the proof of his desire. "You don't need words. I understand completely." And she did. It was the same for her: magical. At once old and new. A sharing that just hours ago she wouldn't have believed possible. Now, through some impossible-to-grasp whim of fate, it was coming true.

Burke's mind echoed the same thoughts. No way had he considered that this evening would end like this. In his wildest fantasies, he couldn't have considered that with one bold kiss, he could have his heart's longing.

He moved into closer, more intimate contact with Emma. This was the moment, the point of no return, beyond which lay heaven on earth for him. He loved this woman so much, and he wanted to show her in the most basic way that she was the only one for him. Now and always.

Emma gasped when she felt Burke begin to breach her barrier. She wrapped her arms tighter about his neck, pulling his lips to hers, caught up in the storm that his movements were unleashing within her. Their tongues mated, as did their bodies, his kiss absorbing her soft cry as they became one.

It was so marvelous to realize that Burke was part of her now, moving in and out, deeper and deeper with each strong thrust. Gradually her body adjusted to the rhythm he set. She matched his movements, meeting him, rocking with the tempo until one final, grand thrust sent her over the edge, spinning out into flames so intense that she thought she'd died, only to be reborn just as quickly.

Burke went with her, soaring into a place brighter and sharper than any he'd visited before, her name on his lips a raw whisper.

Drained, he collapsed against her neck, his breathing ragged. A long moment passed until he managed to raise his head and look into her flushed face. He couldn't believe the peace, the serenity that he saw there.

"Oh God," Emma murmured, her eyes meeting his. "Thank you."

Humbled by her words, Burke could only utter in response, "It's me who should be thanking you for bringing me back to life. For showing me that dreams are possible." He rolled off her, moving so that he lay next to her, his head propped on one palm, the other hand gently stroking the damp, reddish brown curls back from her forehead.

Emma, her breathing gradually returning to normal, stared into his dark eyes. She lifted one hand and caressed his face, the strong blade of his nose, the curve of his wide mouth, his ears. They were all hers.

At least for now, a voice inside her whispered.

She didn't care. She'd shared the most basic, most intimate act that two people could, and she would never regret that. How could she ever regret discovering heaven?

It had been rash, impulsive, unplanned.

It had been beautiful, intoxicating and unpredictable.

It had been more than she'd dreamed and wilder than she'd ever imagined. Even now, with her body slightly sore from the new experience, she couldn't wait to do it again.

But first she had to know what it meant to Burke—and where they would go from here. "We need to talk," she whispered.

Like an arrow straight to her heart, his devastating smile scored a bull's-eye. "I agree," he said. "But not now. Rest." He rearranged their bodies, drawing her into the circle of his arms, her back flush against his chest. He could feel the silk of her stockings against his legs. "We'll have time to talk later. I promise."

"Then you're not leaving?" Her tone conveyed her worry.

"Not right now, darlin'," he whispered, drawing the white sheet over their damp bodies.

His words comforted her, as did the secure feel of his warm body next to hers. She felt safe, cherished. It was there in the weight of his arms under her breasts. She wrapped her own about it, one hand tracing the contours of the thick bracelet on his wrist.

Her own wounded warrior. Emma hoped that she had given him a measure of peace, of the happiness he'd bestowed on her.

He was right. They could talk later.

Sunlight streamed through the sheer curtains and flooded the room with a golden glow. Emma had gotten up earlier as dawn lit the sky and had pulled back the drapes, permitting the sun to come in. As soon as she had, Burke had awoken, calling her name softly. "Come back to bed," he'd demanded.

She had, eagerly, snuggling into his waiting arms, falling asleep again quickly.

Now, as daylight flooded every corner of the room, she was awake. She studied him as he lay sleeping, absorbing every detail from the dark shadow of beard that lined his cheeks and jaw to the soft, thick lashes that fanned his eyes. This close, she could detect the almost imperceptible freckles that dotted the bridge of his nose.

Emma couldn't resist pressing her mouth to those tiny specks of color. They gave his face a boyish, vulnerable quality that made her smile.

Burke awoke, his arms going about her, lifting her to his chest. "What a way to start the day, darlin'."

"My own patented formula," she said, pressing other kisses to his cheek and the tip of his nose.

"One that I could get very used to," he responded, bringing her mouth to his.

Emma surrendered to the pressure of his lips, opening her own to the erotic enticement he provided.

When, a long time later, their lips parted, Burke pulled her head to his shoulder. "I'm hungry," he said. "What about you?"

"Yeah, I guess so," she mumbled, briefly taken aback by his comment.

"Then what say we order room service?"

"Okay." Emma loved the smell of Burke's skin, loved inhaling his scent. She slid one hand over the planes of his chest, again enjoying the feel of his smooth flesh. Talk about getting used to something, she thought lazily. Waking in Burke's arms, his muscled body close to hers, his kisses hot and eager on her lips, was something she could get very, very used to.

They lay together for a few minutes more, each content to linger, until finally, Burke asked, "Who's calling?"

Emma yawned. "You. I want to take a quick shower."

He considered that for a moment. "Maybe you'd better make the call," he suggested. "After all, this is your room."

"Fine," she murmured, thankful that he was concerned about her reputation with the hotel staff, a reputation she hadn't even thought about. It was a lovely gesture on his part. She didn't care right now who knew there was a man in her room, however. In the afterglow of the night they had shared, she had little concern about anything except figuring out where they went from here.

She scooted away from him, pulling the sheet around her body, and edged toward the phone. "Anything special you'd like?"

Just you, he wanted to say. *Again and again.*

"How about eggs?"

She nodded and picked up the phone, tapping out the number for room service. "Good morning, this is Miss Cantrell in Room 505. I'd like a very large pot of coffee and two cups, two orders of *huevos rancheros,* one order of bacon and a basket of biscuits and jam. Got that? Good. Now, when can I expect it?" She listened for a second, then held her hand over the receiver. "She said they'll take almost a half hour or so."

"Okay by me," Burke said, shrugging his shoulders.

"That's fine," she told the clerk. "I'll expect it then."

Emma hung up the phone. She should get out of bed and take a shower, but was stopped by a latent surge of modesty. She was naked beneath the sheet, save for the black, thigh-high stockings she still wore, which seemed somewhat decadently delicious under the circumstances. Burke had certainly seen all there was to see of her body, touched all there was to touch. It shouldn't matter that she was nude.

It was just that this was all so new to her.

Burke saw the blush rising in Emma's cheeks as she sat there, the sheet clutched protectively to her bosom. Swiftly deducing the reason, he shifted, turned his back to her, sitting up on the edge of the bed. He would happily give her the space she needed, he decided, his thoughts unknowingly echoing her own: *It was all so new to her.*

Damn, he thought. It was all kind of new to him, too—being intimate with a woman after so long alone.

A worried frown wrinkled his brow. Had it been good for her? A woman's first time was special, and since she'd waited so long, he wanted it to be all that she'd hoped and more. Was that asking too much? Had he failed her in any way?

Could Emma tell that he hadn't held anything back? He'd given her more of himself than he'd ever shared with anyone.

Burke heard the bathroom door click shut and he rose, picking up his scattered clothes. He looked at the collection and placed it on the back of a nearby chair. The only article he retained were his cotton shorts. Donning them would be expected.

But did he want to?

He listened as the shower roared to life. His body did likewise as he imagined Emma in there, water lapping her lush form.

A smile curved his lips. He added the undershorts to the pile of clothes. No use putting them on; he'd just be taking them off again.

Emma soaped her skin, the scented lather washing away the traces of Burke that lingered. It could never, however, remove the feel of him. That was indelible, an inescapable part of who she was now, who she would be in the future.

She heard the door open.

She watched as the curtain parted.

"May I join you?"

Emma swallowed, the water cascading down her body. "Please do," she said softly.

They sat, finishing the remains of their breakfast in companionable silence. Burke wore one of the hotel's thick, terry robes. Emma had put on her nightshirt, along with a wide smile of contentment. The shower scene danced in her memory. Getting clean had never been so much fun, or such an experience. All her inhibitions had floated away on a sea of sensual pleasure.

Burke was the lover she'd waited so long for. Aggressive and patient, tender and demanding, he was a compelling blend of everything she'd dreamed of. His lovemaking had been a spark to her soul, producing an answering response so deep, so intense that she couldn't bear the thought that she might have to do without it after today.

So far they'd postponed the talk that she knew they must have. She hoped that this meant as much to him as it did to her. If not...

Oh God, it has to mean more to Burke than a simple one-night stand, she prayed. More than a quick conquest, an easy way of jumping back into the saddle. If that's all it was...

Last night she'd acted on sheer instinct, giving herself without reserve to the man she loved. No promises. No declarations. No strings. It had come straight from her heart, a gift for him, wrapped in the ribbons of her love.

Was it too much to expect that her gift would be cherished and valued as something more than just the end of a pleasant evening?

Burke drained the remains of his coffee. "About last night," he began.

Emma put down her cup. She raised her chin and faced him, her eyes locked with his. "Yes?" she answered softly.

"I want you to know..."

"What?"

"That I didn't plan on this happening."

Was there a trace of regret in his voice? she asked herself, wondering if she could be wrong. "Are you sorry that it did?"

"Shouldn't I be asking you that question?" he queried.

"You could," she suggested.

"And what would you tell me?"

"The truth, Burke. That I have no regrets about being with you. None whatsoever." There was no reason to hide or deny what she felt any longer.

"You don't?"

"That's right." Emma wet her lips, her teeth worrying her bottom lip. "I could have said no if I'd wanted to."

He considered her response before asking, "Why didn't you?"

"Because I wanted you."

Burke's body reacted to the simple statement. Hunger rose within him at her honesty. "So where do we go from here?"

Hope rose in her heart, filling her with a sweet joy. She stared at his dark brown eyes, drowning in the heat of them. "I don't know," she replied. "Where do you want us to go?"

"What if I said back to bed? Then, later, back to the Encantadora?" he proposed. "What would you say?"

"That I could be very easily persuaded to the first."

"And what about the second?"

"It depends on what I'd be going back as."

"What about as my wife?" It just slipped out. He hadn't meant to be so quick about it, so direct.

Emma blinked in surprise. "Your wife?" To hear him say the words she wanted to hear, yet didn't expect, was astonishing. "You want to marry me?"

"Yes," he declared. There was no use pretending or holding back now.

Emma was stunned. "Why?"

"If I answer that, I've got to have your promise to answer something for me."

"What?"

"I want you to tell me why you really broke it off with Clay."

"Because I wasn't in love with him, as I told you," she answered. "And I never will be.... Okay, I gave you your answer. Now I want mine."

"Because I can't imagine life without you anymore. It's as simple as that."

Emma swallowed. "You can't?" Her heart was pounding.

"Not since that first night, I think."

Was he actually admitting that he loved her?

"Could you love someone like me?" he asked.

She responded honestly. "I already do."

It was Emma's turn to watch as surprise washed over his face. "You do?"

"I have since I first painted your face," she said, rising from her chair. "Hold on, I want to show you something."

Emma went to her suitcase, stashed in the closet. She bent down and pulled out a small leather portfolio from an inside pocket. He would know how she felt, she hoped, as soon as he glimpsed the sketches inside.

She walked back to where Burke sat, waiting. She unsnapped the lock on the leather folder and handed him the sketchbook.

He took it and flipped through the pages, which were filled with his likenesses—replicas of his face drawn in pencil, in charcoal, occasionally in pastels. He was flattered and stunned.

"At first it was my imagined ideal—a face that came to me in a dream well over a year ago," Emma was saying. "Then the image grew stronger, more insistent. When I saw you that day at the ranch, I couldn't believe it. I thought fate was playing a bizarre joke, until I realized later that you were what I'd been looking for—" she moved to stand in front of him "—whom I'd been waiting for. Last night only proved that to me."

Burke rose and pulled her gently into his arms. Emma rested her head upon his chest. "I love you, Burke."

He spoke the words she wanted to hear. "And I love you, Emma. More than I thought possible." He bent his head and kissed her mouth.

When the kiss ended, it left them both hungry for more.

"I didn't think I'd ever say that after what I went through with Jessie's mother," he admitted candidly. "I thought that chapter of my life was best put aside. Love, to me, was something that happened to others. In too many cases it was sex dressed up in fancy duds, that's all. I wasn't falling into that trap again."

Burke sat down, pulling Emma onto his lap and cradling her. He explained to her about his sustained celibacy, and about his initial skeptical reaction to her coming to the ranch. "But then I discovered that you were the woman who'd done my painting and I got to know you, and I realized how wrong I'd been. By then I was already in love with you."

"What do we do about Clay? I don't want to hurt him any more than I already have," Emma said, her arms about Burke's neck, hugging him close.

"We tell him the truth. I trust that one day he'll share our joy," Burke stated. He hoped that would happen. He loved his older brother, but he couldn't give up the woman he loved now that he knew she shared those feelings. "Anything else?"

"Jessie. Your parents."

Burke replied, "My daughter's a big fan of yours already. I don't think you have much to worry about on that score. As for my parents, they were ready to welcome you before."

"But that's when they believed I was going to marry Clay. Don't you think they'll find it a bit awkward when we tell them we're together?"

"I love you, Emma. They'll understand, I promise."

"Say that again."

"What? That they'll understand?"

"No," she said, raising her head to look into his eyes. She saw the smile on his face as their gazes connected.

"That you love me," she demanded. "When I hear that, I can believe anything is possible."

"I'll be happy to," he said, cupping her cheek, whispering the words in English, and for good measure, in Spanish as well. "All the days of our lives."

Epilogue

The late afternoon sun, pouring in from the windows and the skylight, filled the bedroom with a warm, golden glow.

The woman in the bed yawned and slowly opened her blue-green eyes. She lifted her left hand from its position on the man's smooth, bare chest, admiring the way the light glinted off the gold in her wedding band.

Emma Cantrell Buchanan.

Yesterday, on Valentine's Day, she'd become Burke Buchanan's bride.

The sunlight also glinted off the dull gold finish of the bracelet she wore, identical to the one on her husband's wrist.

Husband.
Commitment.
Family.
Career.

What wonderful words. She had them all now.

Emma's lips curved in a secret smile. And there was something else she had, too—Burke's child growing inside her.

She couldn't wait to tell him. It was her wedding gift to him, an announcement she wanted to make when they were alone. Last night there hadn't been time, for as soon as they'd arrived at her house in the mountains of New Mexico, Burke had whisked her off to bed.

Not that she was complaining. Far from it. She reveled in their lovemaking, in the tenderness they shared, in the closeness of their souls.

Emma loved this man with a passion unsurpassed by anything else.

And she knew that Burke felt the same. It was in the way he made love to her, in the way he held her, kissed her. It was there in the depths of those sloe-dark eyes. It was there in the little things.

And most of all, it was there in his smile—that precious quirk of his lips that now manifested itself, more often than not, in wide, happy grins.

It had been a lovely ceremony. An intimate family wedding there on the ranch. Drew had acted as best man and Vicky as maid of honor, with Jessie as bridesmaid. Only one member of the Buchanans was missing. Clay had sent his regrets—business had kept him away.

Emma regretted his decision, but she accepted it. Time, she was sure, would heal the breach. She certainly hoped so. She wanted Clay to be as happy one day as she and Burke were. She knew Burke wanted it as well.

She'd told Clay just that when she phoned him after she and Burke returned to the ranch before Christmas. It had been an awkward call, but one she'd needed to make. Emma realized that she owed Clay honesty regarding her feelings for his brother. Nothing less would suffice. Clay listened and politely wished her congratulations, which had been more than she expected to hear.

Just last week, Emma had seen a picture of Clay in the *Houston Chronicle* attending a party with a lovely young woman on his arm. Obviously, he was moving on with his life.

"Mornin'," a darkly masculine voice whispered.

"So you're finally awake," she said, scooting backward and resting her head once more on her own pillow.

"I'm awake and I'm up," he growled.

Emma laughed at her husband's remark—the universal laughter shared between lovers. "Well, darlin'," she drawled, mimicking his accent, "you'll notice that it's way past morning. I'd say it's closer to three o'clock, actually."

"Guess I'm plum wore out, sweetheart, from all that exercise I been getting."

"So much for the myth of young Texas studs," she teased, running one hand across the navy blue sheet that stopped at his lean waist.

"Come here, *darlin',*" he responded, "and I'll happily show you the truth in that myth."

"No need," she said, snuggling against his warm body. "I already have proof."

He grinned as he took her hand and laid it against him. "Proof enough?"

"That's not what I meant," she said, giving him a slight squeeze.

Burke raised a dark brow. "It's not?"

"I'm pregnant."

Burke's eyes narrowed consideringly. "Are you sure?"

"No doubt."

"When is it due?"

"Sometime after your birthday."

"September," he murmured.

She nodded. "Are you pleased?"

Burke angled his mouth and took her lips in a deep, satisfying kiss. "Does that answer your question?"

"I'd hoped that you would be."

"How long have you known?"

"Would you laugh if I said almost from that first night? It was too magical not to produce a child. As for how long I've really known, about two weeks."

"And you never said anything?"

"I didn't want this to be a repeat of your first marriage, Burke. When we said our vows, I wanted them to be because we loved each other, not because of the baby."

"God, woman," he whispered against her long curls. "Do you know how much I love you?"

Emma kissed his mouth. "I think I have an idea."

"Well, just so you don't forget," he said, "I want you to know I can't imagine my life without you in it. What I had before—that was merely existing. It wasn't living. I was just going through the motions. What I had inscribed in your bracelet is the truth."

Emma, Only you. Love, Burke.

Emma's lips curved in a deep smile. "Only you, Burke," she said softly as she repeated the words to him. "Only you, my darling," she vowed. "For now and always."

* * * * *

COMING NEXT MONTH

#1039 MEGGIE'S BABY—Cheryl Reavis
That Special Woman!
Reuniting with her lost love, Jack Begaye, gave Meg Baron everything she dreamed of—a husband and a father for her unborn baby. But would their newfound happiness last when Meg's past threatened their future?

#1040 NO LESS THAN A LIFETIME—Christine Rimmer
The Jones Gang
Although Faith Jones had loved Price Montgomery from afar for years, she never dared dream that he'd return her feelings. Then a night of passion changed everything—and Faith wouldn't settle for anything less than a lifetime....

#1041 THE BACHELOR AND THE BABY WISH—
Kate Freiman
Hope Delacorte had one last chance to have the baby she so wanted, but there seemed to be no prospective fathers in sight...unless she turned to friend Josh Kincaid. He'd offered to father her child—no strings attached—but that was before they started to fall in love.

#1042 FULL-TIME FATHER—Susan Mallery
Erin Ridgeway had just given Parker Hamilton the biggest news of his life—he was the father of the five-year-old niece she had been raising. Suddenly, being a full-time father and husband started to sound very appealing to Parker....

#1043 A GOOD GROOM IS HARD TO FIND—Amy Frazier
Sweet Hope Weddings
Country doctor Rhune Sherman certainly met his match when Tess McQueen arrived in town. But she had a score to settle, and he didn't want to think about the raging attraction between them—until the good folks of Sweet Hope decided to do a little matchmaking!

#1044 THE ROAD BACK HOME—Sierra Rydell
When Billy Muktoyuk left home, he impulsively left behind his high school sweetheart, Siksik Toovak, the only woman he'd ever loved. Now he was back—and there wasn't anything that would stop him from winning back her heart.

Silhouette

SPECIAL EDITION ™®

An invitation to three

Sweet Hope Weddings

from Amy Frazier

Marriages are made in
Sweet Hope, Georgia— where the
newlyweds-to-be are the last to find out!

New Bride in Town
(#1030, May '96)

Waiting at the Altar
(#1036, June '96)

A Good Groom Is Hard To Find
(#1043, July '96)

❤❤❤❤❤

Marital bliss is just a kiss away!
Celebrate the joy—only in
Silhouette Special Edition.

SILHOUETTE... Where Passion Lives

Add these Silhouette favorites to your collection today!
Now you can receive a discount by ordering two or more titles!

SD#05819	WILD MIDNIGHT by Ann Major	$2.99 ☐
SD#05878	THE UNFORGIVING BRIDE by Joan Johnston	$2.99 U.S. ☐ $3.50 CAN. ☐
IM#07568	MIRANDA'S VIKING by Maggie Shayne	$3.50 ☐
SSE#09896	SWEETBRIAR SUMMIT by Christine Rimmer	$3.50 U.S. ☐ $3.99 CAN. ☐
SSE#09944	A ROSE AND A WEDDING VOW by Andrea Edwards	$3.75 U.S. ☐ $4.25 CAN. ☐
SR#19002	A FATHER'S PROMISE by Helen R. Myers	$2.75 ☐

(limited quantities available on certain titles)

TOTAL AMOUNT	$_____
DEDUCT: 10% DISCOUNT FOR 2+ BOOKS	$_____
POSTAGE & HANDLING ($1.00 for one book, 50¢ for each additional)	$_____
APPLICABLE TAXES**	$_____
TOTAL PAYABLE (check or money order—please do not send cash)	$_____

To order, send the completed form with your name, address, zip or postal code, along with a check or money order for the total above, payable to Silhouette Books, to: **In the U.S.:** 3010 Walden Avenue, P.O. Box 9077, Buffalo, NY 14269-9077; **In Canada:** P.O. Box 636, Fort Erie, Ontario, L2A 5X3.

Name:_____

Address: _____ City:_____

State/Prov.:_____ Zip/Postal Code:_____

**New York residents remit applicable sales taxes.
Canadian residents remit applicable GST and provincial taxes.

Silhouette®

SBACK-JA2

This July, watch for the delivery of...

An exciting new miniseries that appears in a different Silhouette series each month. It's about love, marriage—and Daddy's unexpected need for a baby carriage!

Daddy Knows Last unites five of your favorite authors as they weave five connected stories about baby fever in New Hope, Texas.

- **THE BABY NOTION** by Dixie Browning
  (SD#1011, 7/96)

- **BABY IN A BASKET** by Helen R. Myers
  (SR#1169, 8/96)

- **MARRIED...WITH TWINS!**
  by Jennifer Mikels
  (SSE#1054, 9/96)

- **HOW TO HOOK A HUSBAND (AND A BABY)**
  by Carolyn Zane
  (YT#29, 10/96)

- **DISCOVERED: DADDY** by Marilyn Pappano
  (IM#746, 11/96)

Daddy Knows Last arrives in July...only from